The Hunted Four

Alex Frew

A Black Horse Western

ROBERT HALE

The Hunted Four

When Walter Watters – aka 'Wattie' – finds out that the hiding place of gold from a major robbery is known to another, he's instantly on the trail. As the sheriff of a small town, he knows that he has to uphold the law. But $2,000,000 in solid gold is a tempting sum. Soon he has to go into an area known as the Wilderness, riding through the monsoon with his companions to where their prize awaits.

But can he trust them?

Worse than that, he is being tracked by a ruthless ex-convict called Kurzwell, who was one of the original robbers. Now, it is a race against time for both groups of men. Only one group can win the prize, but only one has a ruthless killer at their helm.

With time and weather against them, Wattie and his companions face death far from home in a desperate struggle against man and nature.

Bolton
Council

Please return / renew this item
by the last date shown.
Books may also be renewed by
phone or the Internet.

HW

Tel: 01204 332384

www.bolton.gov.uk/libraries

ISBN 978-0-7198-2487-6

The Crowood Press
The Stable Block
Crowood Lane
Ramsbury
Marlborough
Wiltshire SN8 2HR

www.bhwesterns.com

Robert Hale is an imprint
of The Crowood Press

Typeset by
Derek Doyle & Associates, Shaw Heath
Printed and bound in Great Britain by
CPI Group (UK) Ltd, Croydon, CR0 4YY

CHAPTER ONE

Walter M. Watters, sheriff of Benson, sat in his office. More correctly, he did not so much sit as sag, and swelter in a wooden chair. The windows behind, to the side, along with the door, were all open but this did not do much to stir the dead air inside the building. The mercury was climbing in the little glass tube enclosed by the barometer on the wall, and it seemed to indicate there was more of the same on the way.

'Hell,' said the sheriff, 'looks like this ain't going to end soon.' He was speaking to his deputy, Tex, a young man whom he had hired just so that he could have someone to do the many odd jobs that needed doing in a railroad town like this.

Especially when crime was on the cards.

'It's not going to end soon, Sheriff,' said Tex a slim young man with very short hair, and who looked permanently surprised and bemused by whatever was happening around him. 'You've been here long enough to know that this is the start of the Arizona monsoon season.'

'I guess I have,' said Wattie. It was not something he liked to think about, especially not right now when his head was fit to burst.

'Right now it's so durn hot because the thunderstorms are on their way,' said the young man relentlessly. He seemed to have a fixation on the weather. 'You know as well as I do what they're like.'

'Sure I do,' said Wattie, 'horrific, that's what they are.'

'Everyone thinks that out here it's just a desert,' said Tex, 'fact is we get seasons just like anywhere else, and when the rains come, boy, they really come.'

There was no arguing with the point. The boardwalks were there for the simple reason that in the rainy season no-one would have been able to walk ten feet in any direction without sinking into the mud up to their ankles. The saloons were built high, with brick support walls and wooden stairs – with rails – that led up to their batwing doors. In the good – not to say sweltering – weather that favoured the territory most of the time, such stairs were, to say the least, inconvenient for those would be revellers, but at this time of year they were absolutely crucial to the business within.

''Sides, I just heard the news about Quinn,' said Tex. 'I hear he's back in town.'

'Quinn?' For the first time in their desultory conversation. the sheriff sat up properly and took notice. 'Davey Quinn?'

'I knew the name sounded familiar,' said Tex. 'You've mentioned him before, haven't you?'

'Guess I have,' said Wattie. His mouth was dry now, and not entirely from the heat. 'Why didn't you tell me sooner, kid?'

'Wasn't sure if it was the guy you were talking about before, and I just heard a couple of the locals discussing him when I was out and about earlier on. Want a java?'

'A java means putting on the stove,' said Wattie reasonably. 'If you put on the stove, the heat in here'll be just about enough to either drive me to the point where I shoot you for doing it, or I collapse into a heap, either way it ain't a good idea.' He gulped down some of the water that lay in a large, almost empty carafe in front of him. With a supreme effort of will, he got to his feet – staggering slightly in the process – and tightened his gun belt. 'Tex, you hold the fort while I go and check out this Davey.'

'Must be bad if you're going out in this.'

'Davey Quinn was a wanted man in his time. He was born in 1850, in Utah, and even though he was fifteen by the end of the Civil War, he had already fought in three battles. He's as mean as you can make them, and he's killed more men than I've shook hands with. He's been in business in this area before – I know he's had a hand in the mining industry – and he's annexed some land for the cattle business too. The trouble is, he's got a mean streak wider than the Grand Canyon, he's touchy as hell, quick to hear an insult and afraid of nobody.'

'Sounds more like a reason to avoid him,' said the young deputy.

'Maybe in the ordinary line of business, but that ain't how it works around here, as you should know.' The sheriff put on his wide-brimmed hat to protect him from the midday sun, and stepped out into the heat of the day.

He looked around at the town with more than a little satisfaction. Most people were sheltering from the shimmering air caused by the noon sun, except for those who had to be going about their business, and this suited him fine.

Benson was a brand new town, it had been founded just a few years before as a rail terminal for the area, taking in all sorts of goods and services, not just for the cattle business, but for other essential goods that could be used in the county. During the building of the railroad, there had been many attacks on the line by different tribes such as the Apaches, who saw – quite rightly – that the coming of the Iron Horse was a threat to their way of life.

Benson, because it had been created for a particular purpose, was laid out in a regular pattern, with a long main street, and with the others at the back following the same grid system. This was most unlike the chaotic patterns of a typical mining town where people usually set up in a haphazard manner around the main utilities.

On his way to The Hanged Man saloon on Fourth Street, which was thankfully not that far from his office, Wattie passed his home, also near the office. It was situated that way so that he could get to work quickly if anything dramatic should happen. He was on duty both night and day. Being a sheriff was a job where you just couldn't rest on your laurels, at least in his experience.

To add to his troubles, a beautiful woman in a red dress came out to confront him. Being accosted by a pretty woman is not something high on the usual list of woes for a man, but in his case it came up quite high on his count of things that annoyed him. He was confronting his wife, who had run out of their own little home. She had obviously been on the look out for her husband, the lawman.

'Cora, good to see ya, honey, but got to go.'

The woman pouted. She was five years younger than Wattie, who was not old, and she had short, black hair, and eyes with pupils that were the same colour. She looked at him in a way that did not brook much in the way of argument, and gave the killer smile that showed her very white teeth.

'Walter, you give me some money, yes?'

'I would if I had some.'

'A huge amount, but I go to my friend's house today, we ladies get together and play the cards.'

'Not Bezique again?' She could see that the word 'no' was trembling on his lips and gave a smile that could only be described as alluring. Despite the heat that seemed to sap the strength out of him, (and not bother her in the least) Wattie could feel a fire rising in his belly that was unrelated to heat around him.

'How much?'

'If you have the twenty dollars, will be much good.' This time he had to make a feeble protest.

'Twenty dollars? Cora, we don't have that kind of money. You know how much I earn as sheriff, I can't keep funding you like this. I just can't.' She pouted as she looked at him, her lower lip trembling.

'Yet is not good for you to treat me like this. I have no fun in this place.' He relented as she knew he would and reached into his pocket.

'Hell, Cora, that's half a month's wages for some people. It's the last time for a while, do you hear me?'

'I hear you, you naughty man, we discuss later when your business is over?' She gave him a smile so full of promise that he felt his pulse racing.

'Yes.' She stood close to him and lifted up her doll-like face so that he could kiss her on the lips, and then she was gone, leaving behind a sorely troubled man.

Wattie had met Cora in a local saloon, in fact, the very one to which he was now heading, The Hanged Man. She was an exotic creature, much given to wearing robes and silks, her job that of an entertainer, and she did indeed have a good voice for the ballads of the day. She was a mixture of Spanish, Indian and other ancestry with a fiery temper and the voice of an angel. He had been taken with her from the very first day they met, as had a number of other men. He even had to fight off a couple of suitors in order to win her heart.

There is no saying quite so profound as 'marry in haste, repent at leisure'. When Wattie had asked for her hand and she had given it so eagerly, he had not even paused to consider that there might be a catch. That catch quickly presented itself in the first three months of their marriage, of which this was the third. Cora could not continue to work in the saloon after she became a married woman, and being a housewife bored her. He had been trying hard to get her pregnant but that – as far as he knew – hadn't happened yet, and his many duties meant that, purely and simply, his wife was bored.

The trouble with his new wife was, that along with her dark beauty, she had inherited the Latin temperament. It

10

was not anything specific that he said or did. If he was home too late or home too early, if he forgot to be thoughtful with her in mind, if he did not buy her a new dress, or he did not appreciate the meal over which she had slaved and a thousand other transgressions, this would bring on a series of screaming matches which usually ended in a door or two being slammed. Or a plate being thrown at his head. She was a handful.

Wattie had been careful with money most of his young life. His new job carried with it a reasonable stipend and he carried out his duties well. This meant that when he married his new wife, he had a sizeable bank balance, yet in the three months he had been married to her she had made a moose-sized dent in his savings. These had, while not huge, been fairly respectable before this time. In short, he realized gloomily as he walked on, if he was going to keep his young and beautiful wife, he was going to need more income than his job could possibly provide.

The Hanged Man soon came into sight. It had stairs, a brick surround at the foot and wooden rails, just to protect it from the forthcoming bad weather. When the rains came the locals liked to forget them by drinking. Mind you, they liked to forget *all* their troubles by drinking, monsoon rains were just one more annoyance in life.

He paused at the steps that led up the side of the building, took off his hat and paused for a moment, thoughts of his money troubles departing as he prepared to meet the notorious Davey Quinn. He mounted the steps, pushed open the batwing doors and went into the gloriously cool interior. A figure was standing at the bar wearing old jeans and a dusty waistcoat, even the back of

11

his large head was familiar to Wattie.

'Davey,' he said, 'this here's the sheriff of Benson, and I've come for you.'

Slowly the figure at the bar turned, hand reaching for the six-gun at his side.

CHAPTER TWO

Henry Kurzwell was in his cell in Yuma prison. He was a mild-looking man in his early thirties with a high, domed forehead, receding hair and a straight nose. If he had been wearing a suit and given the use of an office, it would have been hard to tell him from one of the pen-pushers who ran the prison. Looks were deceptive. When he had first arrived at the prison, he had been picked on by one or two of the more violent inmates keen to show that they could dominate him. One man had ended up in the infirmary with a few broken bones. The other had tried to make a break for it during routine work outside the prison. He had been shot dead by the guards. Kurzwell had been whispering to the man regularly just a couple of days before, egging him on to make the big break. The man, his ego bolstered, had done just that with predictable results.

The cell door opened with a clang and the governor himself walked into the cell. He was a middle-aged man who looked grateful for the coolness of the stone interior.

'Well, Henry, it's time for you to go.'

'It sure is, Governor.'

'Well, you've been here two years, and for most of it you've been a model prisoner.'

'Thanks, Governor Anson.'

'There was that incident at the beginning where I had to put you in the dark cell.' The Dark Cell was one of the worst punishments in the jail, a stone-lined hole in the ground without a light to relieve the darkness. Prisoners were often incarcerated there for ten days or so with just a little food and water until they saw the error of their ways.

'I guess I had to see the error of my ways,' said Kurzwell mildly.

'Well, you did us a favour in the end. The prisoner you attacked never caused us any trouble again.' The governor gave a nod of his head and the guard bent down, took out a key and unlocked the shackles that enclosed Kurzwell's ankles. Most of the prisoners had a ball and chain when they were out doing construction work, but the high risk ones were shackled all the time.

'Henry, you're a capable man. I don't know what kind of brainstorm took over to make you commit that robbery. I have a proposal to make. Stay here and help me with the administration of the prison. You have a brain in there, unlike some I've had to deal with. I've seen you help other prisoners with their letters. You're an educated man. Stay with me and you'll have a good job.'

'Governor Anson, let me think it over. I have to go and see some – relatives – over in Tucson,' said Kurzwell.

'Well, don't think it over for too long. I need a good

14

man like you.'

'Thanks, Governor, that means a lot to me.' Kurzwell did not add that he'd had enough of Yuma prison to last him several lifetimes, and that the governor could take the straight road to hell, even though this was in his thoughts.

Kurzwell left the prison a short while later. He was wearing a grey suit and had twenty dollars in his pocket. He was indeed heading for Tucson, but only to meet up with two men he had met in prison. Not ex-convicts – he didn't trust other cons because they were too disorganized most of the time, not because of their crimes.

He arrived at Tucson a day or so later, his trip made easy by the new rail system that linked so much of the country, and met up with the guards who had started off their acquaintance with him by guarding him in Yuma.

There was one John Hardin, a big man who carried himself with an air of easy authority. He had an almost casual brutality about him and was ever ready to hit a man between the shoulder blades with the stock of his Winchester '73, or take a prisoner's legs out from under him with a club. He was only in his twenties but had a cynical air about him, and a sceptical attitude that Kurzwell liked.

The other man was nicknamed 'Mule', his real name being Dobbie Dobbins. Mule was not the brightest of men, but he was handy with a club, and a rope, and he too had no problem brutalizing the prisoners under his care. As far as he was concerned, once they were locked up they were fair game. He was overweight, with pasty skin and little piggy eyes.

They were in a local bar where they had arranged to meet, and Kurzwell concealed his pleasure at their arrival.

'Boys, good of you to turn up.'

'We're only here for one reason,' said Hardin, 'you promised a real good reward if we get into this deal.'

'That's right,' said Mule, who usually took the lead from his companion.

'Boys, what can I say.' Kurwell passed them the beers he had ordered on their arrival. 'The authorities grossly underpaid you in there. What were you getting? Eighty dollars a month?'

'Seventy-five,' said Hardin. 'All right, we got somewhere to live, but it wasn't, and isn't enough considering the job.' He narrowed his eyes as he looked at Kurzwell. 'You better have something good for us, else it's over before it's begun.'

'Boys, boys.' Kurzwell spread out hands that had been hardened by construction work during his two years inside. 'Inside' was a joke, because he and many other fit prisoners had spent much of their waking hours labouring to build new cells for the ever increasing population of cons, and quarters for the guards as the prison was extended.

'How's about this?' Kurzwell had been to his secret cache already, just before their meeting. He handed them both a sheaf of notes. Small denominations to make it more impressive. 'Two hundred dollars each, and all you have to do is help me track down some lost property. More as we go on. What do you say, boys?'

The guards looked at the money with a sort of numb

joy. And there was more to come. But Hardin was suspicious.

'I don't know. If it's worth this much to you to get us working, there's a lot more in it for you.' He looked as if he was going to push the money back across the table. Mule would follow suit if that happened.

'I'm not going to kid you guys, it's going to be hard and tough, but I've heard rumours that some roughneck is after the same thing. We have to act now or not at all and that's a sign of how much it's worth to me. If you're not in I'll find others, but I ain't hanging about.'

The two guards looked at each other. Hardin broke the silence.

'The hell with it. We're in.'

Barony J. Coyle – also known as Ony – was in his hotel room at just about the same time as Wattie was approaching Davey Quinn. He was alone in his room, but not really on his own purely for one reason; on the far side of the brown painted door were three people who wanted to have a word with him. He was not particularly anxious to speak to *them*.

'Let me in, you so-and-so,' boomed the voice of Big Bill Toomis. Ony's anxiety not to confront this particular individual was easy to understand. Big Bill was also known as the Benson Bruiser. He was over six feet tall and looked, as he had often boasted, that while he was still in his youth, he could grab a steer by the horns and wrestle it to the ground with his bare hands.

Big Bill had the misguided notion that Ony had tricked him out of some rather large sums of money while they were playing cards. Even though this was not the case, due to the fact that Big Bill was a poor gambler, with a far from poker face that could have been read by a one-eyed man from sixty paces, Ony was still not anxious to face Bill. The bruiser was an individual who not only had fists of iron, but weapons made of that actual material, namely his two six-guns.

Having one person after him was bad enough, but the chorus was taken up by two female voices, that of Dolores and Cha-Cha (not her real name).

'Let me in,' said Dolores. 'I want to speak to you, BJ. And you get out of my way,' she added, speaking to the bruiser who was trying to get there first.

'I will rip your eyes out,' added Cha-Cha who was an attractive Latino dancer in the chorus, nearly as tall as he was, which was not hard given that he was of medium height, and of a slim build that fitted well into his dark suits and fancy waistcoats. 'Let me in.'

'Be with you in a minute,' said Ony a little breathlessly, given that he was shoving some essentials into a carpet bag, including a bottle of whiskey and a bundle of dollars that would have choked a mustang. 'Let's settle this real peaceably,' he added as he briskly opened the window and tied a sheet to the metal frame of his non-too-comfortable bed. 'Be right there, folks, just ease up on the histrionics.' He said this loudly as he dropped his bag to the dusty ground below, hoping that his dulcet tones would have concealed the thud as it landed. In short order, even as he was speaking his final words, he hopped over the sill, saying an inward prayer that the fabric would hold, and scrambled down the makeshift rope. He got to the end, finding that his legs were still at least seven feet off the ground. Luckily the boardwalk had ended at this point. Cursing the effect that the dusty ground would have on his suit, Ony let go.

'Ladies, step back, this one is mine,' said Big Bill. He gave the door a kick that made it resound in its frame, and then blasted a bullet into the lock. He kicked again, and this time the door swung slowly open. Big Bill wasted no time, but stormed inside the room, followed by the two ladies of the chorus. Dolores grabbed at his gun hand but he brushed her off like a particularly attractive fly. He rushed over to the window and leaned over.

'Where are you, ya varmint?' he yelled at the top of his voice, but beyond the sizeable dent in the ground where a body had recently landed, and some dusty marks where he had rushed around the building, there was no sign of the room's recent occupant.

Ony had vanished off the face of the earth.

CHAPTER THREE

Davey's fingers twitched at his side out of habit as he turned but instead of drawing his worn Colt .45 – worn because it had seen a lot of action – he looked at Wattie with a grim visage. Davey was not a pretty sight. At one time his jaw had been broken and his nose too. His nose was a traveller like Davey – it wandered all over his face. He had thinning hair too which only accentuated a look that promised trouble to whoever might want to interfere with his business. Then his mouth opened and he gave a wide grin that was possibly more frightening than his usual expression, showing a set of broken teeth that would have been better kept hidden.

'Wattie, well, dang my hide, it really is you.'

Wattie almost laughed out loud, but managed to retain some sort of self-control.

'Davey, you mean-looking son-of-a-rattlesnake, what the hell are you doing here, of all places?'

Davey looked around at the bar. The place was well-frequented given the outside world was such a hellhole. 'Come with me, to the back of this joint. I've got something we need to talk about.' He ordered another round of suds, and they carried their beers to a table well away from any light that might be glaring through the not-too-big windows.

Only one figure sat at the back, almost obscured by the shadows, and he looked vaguely familiar to the sheriff. But since he had other issues to deal with, Wattie quickly forgot about the man sitting there.

They sat easily across from each other. Davey and Wattie had grown up together, and Wattie could remember some of the wild adventures they had been on when they were young. Davey, just a few years older than his compatriot, had already been through the Civil War when he returned home and recruited his fourteen-year-old companion to help him make a living, mainly by stealing horses and reselling them. Luckily only Davey had been caught at this activity, and Wattie had escaped with only a reprimand for being seen with, and presumably assisting the older boy.

Wattie had never forgotten that Davey had taken the punishment due to them both even though Davey had misled his young companion in the first place, and he had always looked out, after that time, for news of his friend. In a way, now that Wattie was a representative of the law, it was a kind of entertainment, because Davey seemed to be a veritable magnet for trouble. He had been involved in gunfights in Tombstone and even as far afield as Dodge City. He had been in Yuma Prison twice, but not for any of the gunfights in which he had been involved, and now he was sitting here looking not that much different from the Davey the sheriff remembered from all those years ago. His hair was greying at the edges and his voice was a little slower, and he was easier on the beer, but that was all.

'I have to say to you, as a sheriff, I ain't too approving of you being around here,' said Wattie. 'Guess I can treat you to a few beers then ask you to be on your way. This ain't personal, you understand, it's just that things seem to happen while you're around, that I'd rather we didn't bring to this here community, Davey.'

'No offence taken, Sheriff, our paths diverted a long time ago so I guess it's a fair comment.' Davey took a long draught of beer, and his companion immediately ordered another. 'But I'm looking for one person in this hell-hole.'

'And who might that be?'

'You.'

'Well, I must say I'm flattered you would go to all this trouble just to see an old buddy.'

'Don't kid yourself, Wattie. We was boys together, but you were just a sap. Far as I was concerned, you were just a way of helping me get money.'

'If that's the way it was.' Wattie was surprised to find his feelings were hurt by this tough-guy talk.

'I got a story to tell you and I'll be real quick. I was in Yuma when they brought in a guy who looked for all the world like one of your intellectuals. Kurzwell was his name. He was tougher than he looked, broke up Boomer, one of the other cons, pretty bad. Broke the man's legs and one of his arms. Far as we was concerned, Boomer deserved it, he was always trying it on.'

'Prisons ain't kindergarten.'

'Whatever, anyways they flung this Kurzwell into the Dark Cell for punishment and when they fished him out he was flung in with me. Man, he was ill in his mind, lay in his bunk and sung in his sleep like a canary. The Dark Cell gets you that way, cos they only give you water the whole time you're in there.'

'That must have disturbed you.'

'Mosta what he said was bullshit, but once or twice he told a little story about the money he had stolen, and the canyon where it was hidden.' Wattie felt a heat steal over him that had little to do with the weather.

'But why exactly would you want to speak to me about some con's stash?'

'It's more than that.' Davey had been speaking in a low voice but now his tones were so low that Wattie had to lean forward to get even a gist of what was being said. 'You know how in 1881, Benson became the terminus for the Sonoran Railroad from the seaport of Guaymas, Mexico?'

'Yep, it's a line built by the Santa Fe railroad company. It's all set to become a major route between Mexico and the United States for however many years.'

'Well, commerce needs money. A gold shipment was sent in the same year to fund the interests of the Mexican government in this area, mainly to do with goods for industry.'

'How much gold?'

'Oh, only a couple of million dollars' worth.'

'Seems a bit crazy to ship that much money in the form of gold ingots, leastways to a place like Benson.'

'You don't know much about the gold standard then.'

23

Suddenly Wattie was being lectured on economics by a man who looked as if he might jump out of an alleyway and hold someone up for a couple of dollars. It was so absurd that he had to suppress a sudden urge to laugh. Davey would not like such an expression of humour, and might take that expression personally, so he managed to control his features.

'So what happened?'

'There was a robbery just outside of Benson, when some of the passengers upped and produced guns. They killed the guards and took the gold off the train to some waiting horses and headed off to the Wilderness.'

'I know this one,' said Wattie suddenly, raising his voice in excitement. 'It was just before I took up post. They was called the Bronco Boys.'

'Tone it down. That's right. Four of 'em led by one Judd Palmer. They took off to the Wilderness all right, hid their loot and made off back to Tucson. Only, Judd got in a quarrel with the law there, who took exception to their behaviour when the gang broke out, the officers shot 'em all dead in the siege. Except—'

'Except one of them got away?'

'Not really, I think Kurzwell was far from the major player. He just handled the horses and the trip, and helped them hide the gold where no-one else would find it in a million years.'

'Except for him.'

'But he said in his sleep exactly where it was, and I wrote it all down at the time on an old bit of buckskin, using some charcoal. I still have it with me. I kept that old bit of skin on me night and day until I was released, pretended to them it was just a wrap around for my hand when I was doing rough work.'

'Didn't Kurzwell ever question you?'

'He sure did, asked me outright what he'd said when he'd been raving after being in the Dark Cell. I just said straight out I couldn't make it out and I'd stuffed my ears with cloth so's to get a bit of shuteye. And then I glared at him like as I said it. He soon left me alone.'

'This gold, it isn't ours,' said Wattie, 'we'll have to return it to its rightful owners.'

'If it's marked.'

'What do you mean?'

'You ain't too wise about these deals, are you? Sometimes a government don't want others to know where their gold came from and they don't stamp it. Word is, these are unstamped ingots just ready for business.'

Wattie digested this inwardly. He was already getting to the stage where he needed money, a situation that was only going to get worse. If the gold couldn't be traced then a sizeable cut would set him up for a long time to come. Or he could declare the proceeds of a robbery to the authorities, which he was supposed to do, and claim a sizeable reward that way too.

'So, the Wilderness. Do you know what you're taking on?'

'I guess I do, Wattie, which is the reason I'm here. This is just too big a job for one man.'

They both knew about the Wilderness, a stretch of territory just outside Pinal County that had been known in the old days as Jackson County. It was an area that was over 5,000 square miles in extent, and held one of the most complicated systems of canyons to be found anywhere on earth. One man, even with supplies, could do very little in such a place. It was questionable if two could do much more.

'I'm sorry,' said Wattie, 'you've made a long trip for very little, Davey, I'm not the man to help you. You'll have to look for partners elsewhere. Thanks for thinking of me. Drink up, and I hope you'll be out of town by sundown.'

'Why? Why're you taking it like this?'

'Because I uster be a cowboy, still am if it comes to that. I know this area, and what you're doing is as good as sending us both to our doom.'

'But there's a way of getting what we need.'

'Sorry, Davey.' Wattie was now on his feet and so was Davey. They were both still talking in low voices as they scowled into each other's faces. Davey's fingers twitched above his holster and Wattie realized that he was in a tight spot. Davey had spilled some very big beans. He might just take out the sheriff on the spot, walk out of here and ride off before he could be caught. When a couple of million dollars were at stake, an old friendship did not always stand in the way.

The gunman had done the same kind of thing before.

The shadowy figure that had been semi-slumped over his beer rose and came forward.

'Boys,' he said, 'I can help you out.'

Ony did not head out of town as might have been expected. For one thing, it was about as hot as it could get, and he felt as limp as an old rag doll. For another, he had a source of protection that those who saw him gambling might not have expected.

He headed for the sheriff's office.

As he ran as fast as anyone could in the heat of the day, he looked over his shoulder. Luckily Big Bill was not the quickest of thinkers and might look in other haunts before he even thought of the gaol. Ony headed down San Pedro street and swung into the building where Tex was sitting.

'Howdy,' said that person amiably, 'what brings you here, friend?'

'The chance of being killed,' said Ony just as amiably. 'Where's Wattie?'

'Oh, he's away on business,' said Tex, 'meeting some roughneck who's been causing trouble. Can I help?'

'Yes, could you lock me in one of the cells?'

'What?' Tex was not the sharpest of intelligences.

'Could you lock me up for a spell?'

'But you ain't done nothing, son.'

'Listen, I know you ain't that well paid. Lock me up for a whiles and there's something in it for you.'

Tex still looked uncertain. 'But Sheriff Walters—'

'Wattie would lock me up in an instant. He's a friend.'

'Not somethin' friends do in my experience,' said Tex. He shrugged. 'I guess there's no harm helping you out.'

The office was quite roomy since it also acted as the local gaol. Wattie would often hold drunks and miscreants there for three days at a time, letting this act as a punishment before allowing them to go. They were not spoiled for a choice of accommodation; the three cells at the foot of the building were just about big enough in size to walk three paces, with wooden cots set into the wall and a bucket for toilet functions. Ony stalked into one of these, and Tex clanged the door shut, locking his new prisoner inside.

'Thanks,' said Ony, he sank down on the travesty of a bed. 'If anyone comes a-calling, just let them know you've got me and they'll have to go away.' He had stowed his carpet bag beneath the bunk and concealed it with the overhanging blanket.

It was wise that he said these words, because in less than five minutes, Big Bill was at the door, with two attractive ladies beside him.

'Let me at him,' roared Big Bill, 'he's got ma money. Ah'll shoot the critter dead.'

'We want heem too,' said Cha-Cha, 'he's-a cold meat.'

'Ladies, gent, I'm sorry, this here man's locked up,' said Tex, 'he's out of your hands now.'

'I'll shoot him dead right now,' roared Big Bill, 'an' take my chances with the jury. That rattlesnake has ma money.'

'Is this true?' said Tex, turning and speaking down the room. But Ony was already fumbling in the breast pocket of his now dusty, crumpled suit.

'Here,' he said, 'here's his damned money. The sore, lying loser.' He flung the bundle of notes out, they were tied with a bit of string. 'Count it, Deputy, give it to him.'

Tex did as he was asked. The bundle amounted to over $300, a hefty sum to lose in any manner.

'Well, is that the amount he won from you?' he asked of the big bad loser.

'Surely is,' said Big Bill.

'Well, take it and get out of here,' said Tex. The big man pocketed the money, but as he heaved his bulk away from the doorway, he turned for a brief moment and looked back at the cells.

'This ain't over yet. Once you're out of here, we'll have a score to settle.'

'I have too,' said Cha-cha. Big Bill took her by the arm.

'Say, little lady, will you join me?'

'I weel.' With her head held high, she went away with her escort.

'How could you, Ony?' asked Dolores, staying where she was for the moment. He did not answer but lay down with his back stubbornly turned towards her. Her blue eyes flashed with annoyance. 'The hell with you anyway, you don't deserve me,' she turned and followed in the tracks of the other two.

Tex sat down in the wilting heat and waited in silence for a few minutes.

'You want out of there, friend?' he asked, but the only answer was a gentle snore. Ony, it seemed, had succumbed to the heat of the day and his exertions by surrendering to the sweet arms of the sleep goddess. Tex shrugged his shoulders and sat down to wait for the return of the sheriff.

CHAPTER FOUR

'Buzz,' said Wattie, saying the name of their new companion.

'Buzz,' whose real name was Charlie, was an unfortunate case. It was commonplace to find him in the local saloons in a haze of alcohol. Buzz had been a herdsman, leading cattle along some of the toughest trails in the territory, and he had sworn each time he came into town that he was going to reject alcohol and never touch another drop. He had done this before with varying degrees of success. The trouble was, he was now completely broke. He had to sleep out in the open, with his bedroll, and hunt his own food or rely on handouts from the rail travellers.

He had even lost his horse because he had sold it to fund his drinking and gambling. But he only gambled so that he could fund his drinking. He was an amiable enough person, and more often than not locals would buy him a drink and listen to his stories, but the stories were always the same and he was running out of good will. Soon his health would be completely ruined and he would become one of those pathetic figures common in every pioneer town, who would be found dead of exposure, and buried in an unmarked grave.

'I can help you, boys. When I was young I took to the Wilderness, I can be your guide,' said Buzz. Davey's gun hand was twitching above his holster again.

'How much did you hear?' he asked.

'Boys, boys, it's all right,' said Wattie, 'come back to my office, this is too public a place and we have a lot to discuss.' He still had no intention of going along with Davey's wild plans but he was the sheriff, and if it came to some kind of showdown, he would have Tex to back him up. 'I have a couple of bottles of whiskey I keep there for this kind of situation,' he said. 'No one's there 'cept Tex, no prisoners in this heat.'

They went down San Pedro street to his office, Davey wearing a scowl that showed he was not entirely happy with the situation. The factor that had persuaded him to go along with the sheriff's wishes was that he and Buzz had not only met before, Buzz had worked for Davey on one of the cattle trails. Buzz was a tall, rangey man, and still had a great deal of the fitness of limb that he had acquired over the years of roping and herding cattle. In other words, on a proposed mission like this, he might turn out to be an asset of some kind.

'See it's like this, I'm in there, broke, and I sees two gents I know talking real low. I sneaks a bit closer and hears you talking about money, so I comes to the conclusion that I has to do something urgent, that I doesn't like doing. I has to get a job.'

'Admit it,' said Davey, 'you were getting closer so that

you could tap us for a drink.'

'That ain't true,' said Buzz with an air of wounded dignity.

'By the way, you can send that deputy of yours out on patrol,' said Davey, 'this ain't getting out of hand any more than it has.'

Wattie remained calm but inwardly he was cursing the fact that Davey had just removed a major defence. Then he decided things weren't as bad as they looked. Buzz was partially drunk, Davey had been drinking a few beers, and Wattie was a fast draw, one of the reasons he had been given the job of sheriff in the first place. And he was still sober. Besides, in the back of his head was the thought of all that money.

'Tex,' he said as the three of them piled into the building, 'I'm just having a confab with these old friends of mine. Ain't a thing happening out there, take a hike for the rest of the day and I'll shout to you if needed.'

'But, boss—'

'I said get on it, boy. Most people told to get the rest of the day off would be away faster'n a scalded cat.'

Tex jammed his hat on his head and scowled, stalking out of the building, but sure he would know what they were up to in the next few days. He hated secrets being kept from him. In his annoyance he had forgotten that there was a voluntary prisoner in one of the cells.

Kurzwell took the next couple of days to prepare for their trip. The first thing he did was to purchase more supplies than the two ex-guards would have thought possible for three men to transport. He also purchased three big

Mexican horses, and three mules, animals who looked stunted beside the horses, but whom he assured them were literally worth their weight in gold. The two ex-guards were the main purchasers of the goods, with the money he provided, because he needed a front for his business. It was around here that he had committed most of his crimes, and he didn't want to be seen out and about Tucson.

Instead he rented a hacienda at the edge of town where he lay low and enumerated their supplies as they came in, keeping an anxious eye on the cost of the expedition. He was fussy about what they bought too, because his funds were limited, a fact he did not share with those whom he regarded as mere pawns in his game.

It was Hardin who raised some doubts one day as he and Mule returned to Hernandez's hacienda with the tools and guns that Kurzwell assured them they would need to get to their hidden goal. They were both sweating from the heat of the day, but this was tempered by the fact that there was a huge downpour of rain and sudden flashes across the sky, while the air was darkened by the thunderclouds, with the thunder rolling in shortly afterwards.

'Hell,' said Hardin as they entered the building, soaking wet from being outside in the rain for just two minutes, 'this ain't good.'

'Put that stuff down and we'll get some hot food,' said Kurzwell.

'I'm having second thoughts about doing this,' said Hardin.

'Me too,' said Mule, who oddly enough was one of

those people who look wet, down at heel and baggy when they are soaked. He was the kind of person who looked a soggy mess, while his companion just seemed damp and annoyed.

'What're you saying, boys?' asked Kurzwell.

'We seen this kind of weather when we was guards,' said Hardin.

'That's right,' ventured Mule, 'we seen it.'

'And what is your point?'

'Well, I've heard tell it's like out there in the tropics, the rain comes down mighty hard in desert areas blown by a wind they calls a monsoon.'

'Yes, that's about right,' said Kurzwell. 'And I won't lie to you. We saw it in Yuma, hell, the river even used to come up and threaten to engulf parts of the prison.

'Remember, we were even moved out to the cells on higher ground because of the high waters?'

'So that's why we got to thinking,' said Hardin. 'Maybes there's a risk involved in going on this trip.'

'You're right,' Kurzwell told them frankly, 'there is a risk. This monsoon season means that the country we're going to will be dangerous. I've bought some of the supplies for that very purpose, the tents and the slicks, the oiled covers for the packs.'

'You lied to us.'

'I've never lied. It was always going to be dangerous. It was the danger that made those outlaws hide the gold there in the first place. They figured if it was hard for them, it would be hard for anybody.'

'Then wait until this here monsoon season's over, we know from what we saw in Yuma that it don't last all that

34

long. A couple of months at the most. We could go at the tail-end when it's all done an' dusted. You'll get your gold and we'll all be safer and a lot richer.'

'That's right,' said Mule, 'and a lot less wet too.'

'We could do that, boys,' said Kurzwell. Inside he was seething with fury that they were questioning his leadership at all. 'Or we could just wait until we get a couple of clear days and get into our business now that we have our supplies. If we wait for weeks – you know what it's like – you start to get antsy and question things. It preys upon your mind. Besides, you're forgetting an important factor.'

'What's that?' asked Hardin a little sullenly, sensing that he was being out-argued for a good reason.

'We ain't the only ones out for this gold. How would you feel if we went out there eventually, at a time decided by the weather, and discovered that every darn ounce was gone, gotten by those who had gone before?'

'You don't know that,' said Hardin.

'Fact is, I heard there was a little rat called Davey Quinn around here not that long ago. He was asking questions about the Wilderness and trying to get finance. Kept it tight as to what he was up to, but he's the fly in the ointment.' Kurzwell stared beyond Hardin out of the open doorway. 'Look, boys, the rain's stopped. It doesn't last long in these parts, and remember we're going to be far down in a canyon system. There's woodlands and caves where we can shelter. It ain't open desert.'

The two men looked at each other and Hardin gave a heave of his broad shoulders.

'I guess Henry's got us there, Mule. Dry yourself off

with some cloth. We're going. Now what about them eats you promised?'

'Ready real soon,' said Kurzwell amiably. Inside, he was feeling far from that way. Once these two had served their purpose and the ingots were loaded, he was going to arrange a little accident for them both. The Wilderness was good for that kind of purpose.

'What are you smiling at?' asked Hardin.

'Just thinking of all that gold,' said Kurzwell, lying.

CHAPTER FIVE

'So, you've got us,' said Wattie. 'What's this precious information you're going to impart?'

'There's other things first,' replied Buzz, 'like you promised a drop of the hard stuff.'

Davey gave a groan at this.

'Can't you see he's out to stiff ya, Sheriff? He'll take what you've got to offer, give a lot of mumbling yammer and depart, leaving you about as wise as you were before, which, judging from this, is about as worldly as a day old chickadee.'

Wattie said nothing, but produced some glasses and a bottle of whiskey from the drawer of his desk and poured each of them a measure. Davey was not so proud that he rejected this overture. Wattie then poured them another measure because they all took it in a swallow.

'Easy on that second one,' he said to Buzz. 'There'll be more where that came from.'

'Thanks.' Buzz took some more and put his glass down. 'Boys, I'll tell you some of what I know. When I came here as a boy I worked for a fella called Jim March.

He's long dead, got bit in the leg by a wild coyote and blood poisoning set in. He was dead within a week. Anyways, March was one of them enterprising kind of men and he decided to set up a cattle business with no more than a horse, a rope and a branding iron.'

'Sounds like what a lot of men did around these parts,' said Wattie.

'Anyways, we went to the canyons of the Wilderness, ten of us, and with all the roping and herding we did, enclosed a whole bunch of cattle in one of the spur canyons. I learned a lot from him, it was a cowboy life all right, sleeping under the stars and branding them steers with the Lazy M irons that he had an obliging blacksmith make right here in Benson.'

'Sounds like a sweet deal,' said Wattie, while Davey scowled impatiently in the background.

'Well, it could've been. The plan was to herd them steers, with that brand burned on their hides to market in Kansas, pasture 'em on the way, and make a real big profit split all ways. The trouble was the ranchers around here didn't see it that way—'

'Imagine that,' interrupted Davey, 'not wanting to see yore profits taken by a bunch of rustling scumbuckets.'

'Ignore him,' said Wattie. 'Go on.'

'Well, we was at the head of Oak Leaf Canyon, near the whole Wilderness system. There was sweet eating for the cattle, and few people. The ranchers bust in on us before we could move out with our herds. Boy, was they vengeful! Only me and Big March escaped. We lived in those canyons for months, eating game and wild fruit. There had been settlers there before, and we had shelter too in

38

the bad weather. I lived there for weeks, then old March died on me when he was bit in the leg, and I headed back to so-called civilization. But I can still remember every nook and cranny of that Wilderness, it's all burned into my brain, see?'

It was the longest speech that Wattie had ever heard Buzz make, and from the light in the man's eyes and the passion in his voice, it was obvious that he was telling the truth. That much seemed to be evident to Davey too, who had the look of a man who had had a sudden conversion on the road to Damascus.

'So you could lead us?' asked that person.

'I could. Now give us another drink.'

'Trouble is...' Wattie looked thoughtful now that the question of Buzz had been settled. His need for the bottle was an item they could discuss later. 'Trouble is, between three of us this looks a lot more likely, but we ain't got the finance to go ahead. What's your total, Davey?'

'Twenty years of work an' devil-all to show for it.'

'What about you, Buzz?'

'I ain't got a bank account and my wallet's emptier'n an old bucket with a hole in it in a heatwave,' said Buzz.

'Then, gentlemen, I guess it's down to me to get some kind of loan,' said Wattie. He was risk-averse, but he also knew that the money to be gained from an expedition to the Wilderness would solve a lot of his problems. 'I'll just have to see if I can get a loan, but the bank will sure think twice about handing me a dollop of cash without collateral.'

In the silence that followed this announcement, all

three heard a loud groan. Davey, who as superstitious as any trail rider, jumped about a foot in the air.

'The hell with it,' said a loud voice as a figure in one of the bottom cells, lost in the shadows down there, came forward and stared at the three men who had turned to look at him. Ony had been asleep in the coolness of his cell and this had allowed his body to stiffen after his earlier exertions. Besides, he had a painful crick in the neck from sleeping at an awkward angle. Davey's fingers once more twitched towards his gun, and he had been drinking.

'What did you hear?' he demanded, but for once the attention in the room was not on the touchy gunman, but between Buzz and Ony, who were staring at each other as if either party had seen a ghost.

'Do you know each other?' asked Wattie.

'I should do,' said Buzz, 'he's my brother.'

'What the hell is *he* doing here?' asked Ony. It was evident that there was no love lost between the siblings.

'I might ask you the same thing, Ony,' said Wattie. 'See, I don't rightly recall locking you up for any reason.'

'That's because you didn't,' said Ony. 'Now how's about you let me out and we talk with each other?'

Kurzwell had a fixed determination about him that neither of his two men could understand. They knew that he wanted the gold that was hidden in the canyon system, but neither of them could really picture in their heads what a colossal sum of money he was talking about. They simply could not understand what it would look like. Kurzwell knew, because he had been there, that three mules were necessary for a simple reason. Gold was heavy. Fortunately it came in the form of ingots, which meant that it could be spilt up and carried easily.

He was urging them onwards for another reason that he did not share with them. Almost all of his money was gone now. He had invested everything in this expedition. An important factor within this was guns. Kurzwell was determined that he was going to take as many weapons as he could. To this end, he armed his men and himself with a Winchester rifle each and a bullet belt to go with it. He also supplied some smaller Smith & Wesson pistols. The big Colt .44 and .45s were great if you had some kind of conflict on the range, but he found the smaller calibre .32s were more useful when you were on the go. Because of their size, these were easier to handle if you were firing and moving. He also supplied the men with plentiful amounts of this type of bullet.

'You expecting trouble?' asked Hardin upon receipt of these weapons. They were setting out now to take the animals and supplies to the Wilderness, their leader had been pushing for it to happen that very day.

'I'm not expecting anything,' said Kurzwell, 'but if there's going to be trouble, we're going to trouble it first.'

'Is it because of the wild animals?' asked Mule.

'What?' asked his leader.

'I heard tell there's any number of things out there that can attack and kill a man, things like coyotes, bears, and bobcats.'

'Don't be stupid,' said Hardin scornfully.

'I think he might just be right,' said Kurzwell, suddenly

41

thoughtful. 'You may mock Mule, John boy, but there are a lot of animals out there, and they're not used to humans. They might just startle easily, killing without a thought.'

'Might be our chance to do a bit of huntin',' said Hardin with a look of relish. 'my brothers have done it, and I fancy bringing down a bear or two.'

'That's all right as far as it goes.' Kurzwell managed to keep the look of distaste from his features. He might be ready to attack anything that attacked him, but he didn't see the point of shooting anything otherwise, unless it was for food.

Mule looked along the length of his Winchester as if he was drawing a bead on the animal in question.

'Bang, you're dead!'

Kurzwell looked at him with some kind of astonishment.

'Right, pack that away, you'll have time to practise when we get there.'

Fortunately the weather had turned again, and the temperatures were down. There was dampness in the air that was not usually present at other times of the year. Soon, in five days or less, they would be at the Wilderness. As they went on their way, Kurzwell grew more optimistic. This had taken most of his resources, but the reward would be great, and that was all that mattered.

Of one thing he was determined. Davey Quinn had run out of a lot of goodwill in the territory, which meant that his chances of getting enough finances to go for the cache were slim, but there was an outside chance that this might happen. Well, Davey would soon find out who he was up against. Kurzwell smiled to himself at the thought. It was not a pleasant smile, either, or one that boded well for anyone who came up against him.

The four men sat around the sheriff's office. Ony was not the least disturbed by Davey's hostility. After the events that had transpired that day, he was ready to take on the disgruntled gunman with information that would be music to their ears.

'Boys, I have a good piece of news for you. I was listening to the – er – discussion between you gents.'

'What do you want?' growled Davey, his battered features more hostile than before. 'I thought this was between me and the sheriff, now it's turned into a damned town meeting.'

'It's all right.' Ony held up his hands. 'I know that you have a little expedition to finance, and I also know that I have something to help you.'

'What?' growled Davey.

'Funds. I can help you out – for a little return on my investment.'

'Like what?'

'Fifty fifty. I provide the funds, you give me fifty per cent of the take.'

'You rattlesnake.' This time the gun was in Davey's hands. 'I'll shoot ya down and then we won't need to give ya a penny.'

'Boys, stop this right now.' Wattie got between the two of them. 'Davey, put that gun away.' Wattie looked sharply at his old friend.

'Davey, this man has money. He's going to help us out.

43

We don't have any. What would you rather do, have fifty per cent of $2,000,000 or the whole of nothing?'

'Yeah, well, he wouldn't be helping you if there was nothing in it for him,' said Buzz. 'Like he couldn't even help his own brother.'

'You're a drunk,' said Ony. 'I don't help drunks.'

'You could've helped me when I needed to get back to business,' said Buzz.

'You'd've taken the money and drank it in a week,' said Ony.

'You don't know that. You could've given me a chance.' This was a reference to a meeting where Buzz had gone to see his brother and asked for some finance to start a livery business right here in town. Ony had refused and had vanished, as was his practice, going on his gambling rounds in different parts of the territory. Now there was a real hostility between the brothers that would not be cured by a simple word or two between them.

'You would've drank it in a week,' repeated Ony, 'besides, you've never succeeded at anything in your life. Look at you; you're crawling inside a bottle right now.' Given that Buzz had poured himself another drink, and had poised his glass to carry it to his lips, there was some truth in this accusation. Buzz put the glass down.

'The hell with it,' he said with simple dignity, 'I don't need this. Find the thing yourselves.' With this, he picked up the glass again, gulped down the whiskey, since he was no fool, and headed for the door.

'Wait, wait a minute.' Wattie stood in front of the doorway. 'If we're going to find this gold, we have to work together. Ony, we're buddies, but I don't want you setting off your brother. Buzz, we're not taking any booze with us, but you'll get all the drink you want when we comes back. You two boys need to work together and leave your differences behind, agreed?' If there was a moment when Wattie decided to go along with the expedition, this was it.

He stood there for a long moment. Buzz allowed the thought of what he could do to settle into his addled brain. You could almost hear the wheels turning and the gears shifting.

'All right,' he said at last, 'I'm in.'

Ony, who had been considering the matter, looked across at his brother.

'All right, fella, perhaps you're useful for something after all. If we need you, we need you.' He kept his voice bland as he said this, and it was obvious that he was holding himself back from further criticism.

'Well, Davey,' said Wattie, 'looks like we come as a package or not at all, what d'ya think?'

'Hell, I didn't know we was going to end up as a gang,' said Davey with a faint tone of despair. 'I guess we can't do this separate now it's out there.' He looked at them sharply. 'But it goes no further.'

Wattie sat down at his desk and pulled out a sheet of paper.

'What're you doing?' growled Davey.

'Writing down a list of what we need, we're kitting up and leaving tomorrow.'

CHAPTER SIX

Oak Leaf Canyon had been given this name for a reason. It was a deep and leafy depression in the earth where all sorts of trees grew in abundance, not just those from which it took its name. Four horsemen arrived riding in a string. They were within the Galiuros mountain range, in the canyon wilderness that bore the same name. The trip here had not been without its troubles, because they had been subject to a number of squalls and even a sandstorm, which luckily had not lasted all that long, but had been enough to show them the power of the weather. They were not to know that Kurzwell and his men were closing in on the same trail.

When the four horsemen arrived, the sky above them was a deep turquoise blue. Oak Leaf Valley seemed to sink deeper and deeper into the earth as they went on. Down the middle was the Galiuro river, a fairly robust stream that had been running here for a million years, carving out the huge valley. Cliffs reared up to either side of them, the trees ranged all along the slopes and growing at sometimes crazy angles to the floor of the valley.

There was something tranquil about the place. Mostly because it was poor country for farming while the loggers had not yet moved in.

'Looks as if it's clearing up,' said Davey almost cheer-fully. This was his life, talking and planning were not his forte, and he much preferred to be out here riding with his companions.

They were carefully skirting along the edge of the river. They had to cross at one point to get to the broad plain of the valley, where the ground was flatter and not strewn with quite so many boulders. Davey fell strangely silent as they did this, for the water was deeper than they had anticipated and it touched the bottom of his feet as he rode. Davey spurred his mount on with kicks to her side and he was visibly relieved when they were at the other bank.

'Been in too many rivers,' he said as he waited for the other three, 'nearly got me too, treacherous things. This is nothing.' But it was clear that he was covering up his fear of fast-flowing water with mere bravado. 'So, how did your missus take it?' he added, distracting his attention from his own fears.

'Cora?' Wattie had just ridden his own grey across the water and was emerging in front of his old friend. He thought then of the slamming doors, the screams, the throwing of objects at his head, and the demands to know what he was doing. Then the assurances he had to make without giving too much away to calm her down, the promises that he was going to make life a lot better

47

for them both, and that he was going to be back soon. The way she had made love to him the night before his departure, and her sullen looks when he was finally leaving.

'She was fine,' he told Davey.

Davey grunted at this. He had a few women scattered up and down the territory. For all his looks he seemed to be attractive to the ladies, but he had never considered settling down with one of them. As the other two arrived, he showed that he had other things on his mind than Wattie's troubles with an ex-showgirl.

'Time to tell you boys something of what I know, so you can see I ain't leading you a merry chase. One of the things ole Henry accidentally told me was about a rope bridge that leads from one canyon to another, seems it was the only way to get across.'

Wattie turned a little pale at this. Davey might not like water, but Wattie had a terrible fear of heights. He didn't mind looking up at mountains but he sure as hell wasn't comfortable climbing, or looking down from them.

The width of the Oak Leaf Canyon was not something that Wattie had expected. He had pictured a series of narrow passageways, with walls that rose for hundreds of feet, perhaps a thousand feet or more, but was instead confronted with a green table where the river spilled over to rich grassland and where other canyons led off the main one. Buzz, who had been silent and morose since they had set out, suddenly give vent to a hoarse cry and rode forward to one of these narrower entrances.

'There she is! That's where we put our beeves. Look, you can see where we built the gates. Took us days to make 'em, but once we had our cattle in there they was snug as a bug in a rug.'

'You would think the cattlemen would make use of a place like this,' said Ony, 'look at the good feeding here.'

'Just one big problem,' said Wattie, 'it's too remote, took us days to get here, what was it, five already? And we're just four horsemen. If it hadn't been for that sandstorm, we'd have made much better time. It isn't like that when you've got thousands of beeves, you're liable to lose many of them on the trip back, there's nothing for them to eat or drink. It's different for the rustlers, they don't care how many they lose, they didn't pay for them in the first place, so they'll always turn a profit.'

'We sure did,' said Buzz.

'Only thing you did in your durn life, and it was crooked,' said Ony, shaking his head.

'Easy, boys,' said Wattie, 'we've got a long way to go. Buzz is going to come up with the goods, ain't you?' But that particular cowboy said nothing.

Davey got off his horse, not ungratefully. He had short legs and the big southern saddles didn't agree with him. His horse, Daisy, a little spotted mare, turned her head disdainfully from him and began to crop at the lush meadow grass.

'Time for me to tell you where in particular we're going,' he said comfortably.

'It was kind of a leap of faith following you here,' said Wattie. 'Only thing that made us do it was your complete confidence, and the certainty you knew what you were doing. A couple times there when them hububs were

49

blowing at us, I thought of chucking it and heading back to Benson.'

He was not the only one who winced at the thought of the sandstorms that had threatened to engulf them on the way here. Luckily these were not as severe as the ones that occurred out at Yuma and Phoenix. Out there, when a sandstorm arrived, it would fill the air with grit, making it impossible to get anything done for up to three days at a time. Out at Gila, the road to the Wilderness, the landscape was more rocky and the storms lasted for only a couple of hours a time. Even so, you had to cover your face, and those of the horses too, to prevent them all from breathing in the fine grit. Yet they all got covered from head to foot in the stuff. The storm halted after an hour, but it was a bad enough experience. The word 'hubub' came from the Arabic word 'Haboob,' and was a local version of that name. It was a hurricane-like wind that arose when a stormhead built up, threatening thunder and lightning, then collapsed. The remaining air that had built up, with nowhere else to go simply ravaged the land, raising huge amounts of sand until it petered out.

It was only Davey's unshakeable belief that they would find their fortune that kept them going, even when they were cursing him for what they had gone through.

'Spill it, friend,' said Wattie, 'and you, Buzz, listen real good.'

'This place ain't empty,' said Davey, 'it never has been, it's about 5,000 square miles, so somebody's going to want to live here. Trouble is, it's too far for easy supplies, it's hard to grow regular crops in big amounts, and if the river floods it cuts off the feed for your beeves and horses.'

'I didn't think we was going to get a lecture on farming techniques in canyons,' said Ony. 'Get to the point, Davey.'

'That is the point.' Davey glowered at Ony as he spoke. It was obvious that he considered the young gambler to be an upstart, only tolerated because of finance. 'Deep in this canyon system there's a place where some settlers from the past decided to have their own little kingdom. They'd built a rope bridge at the top of a low peak, and once across, that was their land.'

'There could be a hundred rope bridges out there for all we know,' said Ony, a trifle scornfully and Davey fixed him with a basilisk eye.

'You just stopped taking your mother's milk yesterday. You don't have a clue what you're talking about. The effort o' making that rope bridge – well it beggars belief. The only reason was, some people are just plain ornery. They want to have their own place and nothing to do with the rest of the world and that's why. Trouble was, the isolation and the weather – the drought – killed off the farmers that built it. Thing is, in the deeps where they lived, that's where the robbers put their little goods, and that's just plain where we're heading.' He stopped talking and looked expectantly at Buzz, as did the rest. By this time, they were all standing in a little group together with their horses cropping at the lush meadow. Buzz did not look happy to be singled out.

'You would have to do that,' he said, 'pick on just about the most difficult place in this system to reach.' He cleared his throat and spat on the ground. 'Sure, I know that area.' They were still looking at him expectantly. He glowered at their eager faces. 'Say, how's a guy supposed to think without a drop or two of the old rotgut?'

'Sensibly,' replied Wattie, 'there's no point drinking until we get there, and find what we're looking for, or of giving you drink in any shape or form until then.'

'Aww, that's not good enough.'

Wattie had to admit that if it had been up to him he would have given Buzz a tipple, considering they were in the middle of nowhere. He also had to admit that the former cowboy was a sorry sight, with dull eyes that seemed to look at everything he saw with no hope, and hands that trembled as he pressed them to his face, which he did far too often for everyone's comfort.

'Just think of what we're doing,' urged Wattie, 'you'll have all the booze you want by the end of this, ain't that good enough for you? You'll be able to set up your own business too.'

'Thought that the money belonged to the state,' said Davey suddenly.

'We'll see about that,' said Wattie comfortably. 'If it's like they said, and it can't be traced, I don't see why working stiffs like us,' he took a sideways glance at Ony, 'well, in your case working is stretching it a bit, but you know what I mean. Why shouldn't we make the effort and get the reward?'

'How far is it to the bridge then?' asked Ony.

'Miles,' said Buzz, 'and it ain't the easiest route, either. We'll have to go through here, down into a slot canyon and back out again where it widens to some hills beside a deep valley.'

'Well, why couldn't we have gone in from a different angle?' asked Wattie.

'Because this is the easiest route,' said Buzz. 'More than that, it's the one I know.' There was no arguing with this. He was their only guide.

'If we make good time in the next couple of days, is there any reason why we can't get there?' asked Wattie.

'None at all,' replied Buzz, but even as he spoke there came a major obstacle to their plans. The turquoise sky above had gradually started to turn grey even as they stood there, a small group conversing with each other. The clouds turned as dark as the underside of a rock, and it began to rain.

This was not rain as you might know it at any other time of the year. Come to think of it, it barely rained in the territory, but if it did it was usually only a brief squall that blew over in minutes. In minutes, this rain showed that it was not here for a brief time at all and was set to continue. For once Buzz took charge.

'It's all right, guys,' he said. 'I know just the place to go.'

They got on their horses and followed in his wake. He seemed so certain of what he was doing that they followed him with a blind trust in his abilities. The rain was unceasing, not particularly cold but steady, coming down in big fat droplets that still, despite the fact they were wet, somehow seemed to have a flavour of the desert about them. Luckily they had all seen the sensible way of doing things and had put on their slicks, but even so their legs and their boots were getting wet, and the droplets managed to find their way into the hoods of the garments and crawl down their necks.

'Hell and damnation,' said Wattie (or words to that effect), 'this is almost as bad as the dust storms.'

The only thing they could do was plod onwards for a period of time that seemed like hours, but could only have been for another fifty minutes at the most. The horses were unhappy, their heads down, their progress seeming to get slower and slower.

Worse still was the effect the rains were having on the Oak Leaf River. It soon became apparent that the low banks of the river were not capable of containing within their bounds the volume of waters coming down from the heavens. As it was, it was not long before the banks were bursting and spilling onto the grass. This had the effect of covering the surrounding meadows to the depth of four or five inches, and swelling the waters of the river considerably. To get away from the waters, this pushed them to one side of the canyon, so that the horsemen were hard up against the trees although not sheltered completely by them because of their erratic growth.

Even Buzz, who seemed sure of what he was doing, got lower and lower in the saddle as they went onwards. Finally he straightened up as he looked ahead. The valley was not entirely clear and it had started to narrow at the point where a spur of rock stuck out from the uneven walls.

'Round here,' said Buzz with a rising excitement in his voice. 'This is where me and March had our cabin. We've got shelter, boys.'

He spurred his horse onwards around the bluff and

the others came after. Dripping wet and dispirited, they all halted beside where Buzz was looking at an object worthy of his despair. There was a building that might have once been described as a cabin, but the twin evils of time and weather had not only rotted the wood of the walls, but the roof, which had been made of grass and wood woven together, had fallen through to what remained of the interior. They might have been able to salvage some kind of shelter out of the remains if it had not been for the way in which the swollen river, which had burst its banks at some previous time, had swept a sizeable amount of mud and loose stones into what was now little more than a pile of rubble.

CHAPTER SEVEN

When Kurzwell and his companions set off, they were in a good mood; the two men because they were the type who liked to get on with things, and because they were greedy, and Kurzwell because he was happy that they were finally on their way.

They encountered some rain and a lot of heat on their journey. It was only after a few days, as they neared their goal, that the first storm overtook them. Only it wasn't a storm, not really. They were plodding across the Gila desert towards the canyon system when the familiar thunderheads built up to the south. They were not unprepared and quickly covered up to meet the rain. However, the clouds roiled away from them, and just as suddenly as taking in one breath and letting out another, the temperature dropped and they could feel the air starting to change. Hardin opened his mouth to speak but he had little chance to say anything before the wind blew across the desert and began to swirl up the sand around them.

Although they didn't know this, they were only a few

hours behind the other expedition at this point, and still had to get to Oak Leaf Canyon. The Catalina mountains arose to one side and the Guilaro peaks to the other, so that they were hemmed in by a chain of mountains to either side. 'Hemmed in' was a loose term when facing such distances, because it would have taken days of riding to get to the foothills of either mountain chain.

'Ride hard, men,' said Kurzwell, urging his own steed forwards even as he said the words.

They were lucky in a sense because they were not too far from a group of large rocks on the path to the canyon. The fine particles of sand soon whirled into the air so that they could hardly see what was in front of their faces. The only way that Kurzwell knew that he still had his followers with him was the fact that the two men were cursing fit to burst, and that their curses were muffled because their bandannas were wrapped around their faces, as was his. His hat, which had a large brim, was pulled down low across his forehead, but even so he could feel the fine grains of sand stinging his eyes. He was not a man who gave in to feelings of self-pity, but at that moment he felt sorry for himself.

After what seemed like forever, they managed to get to the rocks. These were big red bluffs that marked the beginning of the canyon trail, big slabs of striated rock that had been carved into grotesque dolmen by thousands of years of wind and rain, and the actions of the earth itself. Given that the sandstorm was coming in from an easterly direction, the only way they could shelter from it was to get their horses to ride in between one of the bigger slabs so that the animals could shelter together, then find another slab for themselves. Matters were far worse than this because they were leading a mule each, loaded down with the necessary supplies; this meant that they had to make sure those animals were sheltered behind a different rock from their horses before they were able to assemble together.

Mule, who had just finished sheltering his own animals including the one he was named after, seemed to be in a particularly stubborn mood.

'The hell with this, I didn't sign up to go through this kinda shit. I'm going back to work in Yuma.'

Kurzwell and Hardin did not speak for a while, both of them feeling the effect of the grit on their faces. And it was still settling down on them as the storm swirled around and around. Neither of their expressions were visible, but Mule could tell from the way Kurzwell stiffened that he was not pleased with the words of his subordinate. Mule said nothing more, for the moment, but pressed his broad back obstinately against the rock as he waited for the storm to abate. As soon as the swirling dust had settled down, Mule took off the bandanna and stared at Kurzwell, who took off his own mask. The two men stepped back from one other, and it was obvious that they were now completely hostile, circling around warily, making sure that the distance between them did not close.

'I shoulda know better than to trust an ex-con,' said Mule, 'you're leading us out here to die. I'll just take my load and get outta here.'

'You think so?' said Kurzwell. 'And what good will it do you?'

'More good than following you, and not knowing what's going to happen next.'

'You want certainty, then you go to a Bible study class,' said Kurzwell. 'You want to gain, you keep on following right behind me. 'Sides, what do you think you'll do out there? Far as I'm concerned, you'll wonder around in a big circle and we'll find your bones on the way back. After you've eaten most of your horse to survive, that is.'

'Why, I'll shoot you.' Mule reached for his gun, only to find that his wrist was being held by an iron grip. He turned to look into the stern, unsmiling face of the man whom he had once considered to be his friend.

'Put it away and act sensible, Mule.'

'He's leadin' us on a wild goose chase.'

'What makes you say that?'

'We've been nothing but rained on since we started, and now this.' Mule shook the front of his thick jacket in disgust and a cloud of gritty red dust arose even though the storm had vanished. 'Look what we've had to put up with already.'

'You think I'm finding it any easier?' grated Hardin from between clenched teeth, but letting go of his friend's wrist. 'What do you get from shooting Henry? A pack full of goods, a mule and a horse, that's what. You go with him, you stand the chance of doing a lot better. You're crazy with the rain and the dust. You just haven't experienced the real world, that's all.'

'The hell with you, I was a prison guard for long enough.'

'What age are you? Twenty-two? Mule, you're young for your age. Henry's given us a chance and we got to take it. See, folks like us, when we get old, if we're lucky enough to get that far, we get flung aside and left to rot. This is our chance and if you can't see through all that, and do what it takes to get you there, I feel mighty sorry for you.'

Mule let this sink in, then glanced over at Kurzwell. The air was a lot lighter by then and the heat of the day had started to fade. They would have to get to an encampment by night anyway and set up their 'A' tents.

'I guess he's right in his way. Johnny's always been a bit of a peacemaker. But this seems to be going on forever, this trek.'

'Right.' Kurzwell looked at his subordinate. 'Fact is, when we hid the ingots, we was expecting to come back and get them in less than half a year. It's been two years now, and a man forgets a lot in that time. I guess I forgot how hard it actually was just to get here. I should have warned you, Mule, or even the both of you. I'm not keeping a thing from you. This isn't easy for a number of reasons. If we fight between ourselves it'll get us nowhere. Let's shake on it.'

'All right,' said Mule reluctantly, grasping Henry's hand and feeling an iron grip that satisfied him the man meant business.

More amicably than before, the men checked their horses then saddled up and rode towards the mouth of the canyon that would bring them more riches than they had ever known. Henry Kurzwell, riding in front of the others, even had a smile on his face. He was picturing what it would be like to put a bullet into Mule's head, and the result pleased him greatly.

*

Ony was all set to heap a load of insults on his brother's head.

'You blasted son of a coyote, you promised us shelter. Your promises are as empty as your head.' But Wattie held up an appeasing hand.

'Ony, now is not the right time. Let's get to some kind of hideaway.' He turned his face to their would-be guide. 'Buzz, do you know of any place nearby?'

''Course I do,' said Buzz, 'I was jest going to suggest an alternative when this jackass set in on me. Place like this, where there's been a lot going on over the years with the land upheavals, there's a lot of caves.' He led them onwards, with Ony still faintly cursing under his breath, and Davey looking like some demon carved out of the surrounding rock with his set face and hard eyes.

Around the bluff and beyond the wrecked cabin, the canyon opened up again. Buzz led them up the sloping sides until they came to what could only be described as a series of irregular stone ledges. Even better, from their point of view, was the fact that the sides of the canyon sloped inwards at this point, showing that the walls had been worn away by the waters that had once flowed through here so many years ago. This meant that once they were under the stone ledges that proliferated so greatly, they were able to shelter the horses. The fact that there was also some rich earth around this area meant that the animals were able to graze by leaning their long necks over so they could crop at the long grass, and the bushes that grew almost to the height of a man.

61

Just to be out of the rain was a blessed relief, but Wattie found to his immense annoyance that he had somehow been cast in the role of leader of their little group. When they climbed from below, the inward slope meant that none of the alleged cave entrances had been visible, but as they left their horses – making sure that the animals were unsaddled and tethered tightly to the nearest branches – he led his companions to a hole in the rocky surface that looked more than a little promising.

The cave entrance was over twenty feet wide and although it seemed a trifle narrow at the front, they soon discovered, as they threw their packs and saddles inside, then followed suit, that it was a sloping entrance that went back at least another hundred feet and widened out too. Because it widened upwards there was also an area that was big enough for them all to stand up.

'First thing we do,' said Wattie, 'is get some kindling.' He did not say so, but he had seen men who were soaked to the skin get cold and succumb to a lethargy that seemed to overtake all their senses, make them lose control of their body functions, just before they died.

He went back out with the rest. Luckily the actions of wind, weather, and the felling of oak trees by these evil twins meant there was more wood than they could gather. The unrelenting rain meant that they got soaked again in the process, but with the four of them working together, it meant that they had gathered enough wood within an hour to do them for days if need be. If they ran out, which was a rare possibility, they had the ability to forage for more.

'Right, boys, the fire's on the go, once it's burning real

hot, get down to yore long johns, we're drying off,' said Wattie.

They soon had a log fire burning at the entrance to the cave, and even made makeshift clothes horses out of brushwood on which they laid their garments, dried them off and got fully dressed again. Only then was it time for them to break out some of their provisions, heat up the water they garnered from deep rock-pools outside and make a welcome pot of java for all.

They sat there around the fire, drinking their black coffee that had been sweetened by molasses, while their shadows jumped and danced around them in the flickering flames. The world outside was grey and dark as the rain cut down on the light of day so it looked almost as if they were in the evening, even though it was only late afternoon. Wattie thought he could hear a papery rustling sound somewhere not far from where they sat, but he dismissed this as only his imagination.

It was not as if a grizzly had come roaring at them when they took up the cave. He had not said so to the others, but this had been his biggest fear. He knew they would have to shoot some animals for food supplies for the trip back, but a bear would be his last choice given the fact they had tremendous claws, huge teeth, and fought back.

'Well, I didn't reckon it would be this bad,' said Davey, looking at the outside world. 'Still, I know this territory, the rains don't normally last that long. We could be on our way tonight.' It was obvious that their target was still uppermost in his mind.

'That might be the case,' said Wattie, 'except this

doesn't look as if it's going to let up soon, and at least we're in a secure place for the moment. I say we wait a day or so after the rain stops and then get back on the trail.'

'He's right,' said Buzz, 'that's the best thing to do.'

'Why the hell would we wait?' said Davey, who was not perhaps the greatest strategic thinker amongst them.

'Because the Galiuros is not just going to be risen for a short while,' said Buzz, 'it's going to be swollen by the rainwater that continues down from the mountains. We'll have to ford the river again at some point to get to Hidden Canyon – the place we're looking for. We've worked together, Davey, you know what it was like crossing the Cimarron and the Pecos when they was flooded. We lost beeves by the dozen, and near enough our own lives.'

Davey paused at this. There was very little in life that frightened or worried him, but he did not like to be caught up in fast-flowing water, having nearly lost his life through drowning when he was young and inexperienced, and roving the cattle trails.

'It's only water,' scoffed Ony, 'we'll get across all right. Look at all the wood we managed to forage for this fire. There's bound to be more than enough to make a bridge for us to get some kind of footing, just sinking it in the water.'

'Know what? You're right,' said Davey. He said this as if he was not entirely convinced, and the others realized that here was a man who was clutching at a hope – however distant – of what he wanted to achieve. 'Trouble is, we can't just lounge about the place and wait for another twenty-four hours.'

'Why not?' asked Ony. 'We're secure enough here. If we wait it out, we'll just have to go to the rope bridge, we'll be able to get across after the river dies down.'

'That ain't the way of it,' said Davey, 'you don't know the half of it, either. I ain't told you folks before, but this Kurzwell. He's kind of mad, and he's on the loose, having ended his sentence. He could well be right on our tails.' There was a silence broken only by the crackling of burning branches, and that strange rustling sound that the others seemed to ignore.

'When the hell were you going to tell us?' asked Wattie.

'Well, I guessed with all the labour of getting across the desert and setting up in this here canyon, that was enough on our plates without worrying you with other details,' said Davey.

'When you say he's mad, what do you mean?'

'He don't care who he hurts to get what he wants. Oh, in Yuma Prison, after a little unpleasantness, he was the governor's blue-eyed boy, even helped bring in some reforms because he ain't stupid. But it's because he ain't stupid we'll have to look out for him.'

Wattie felt a sudden chill go through his veins that was quite unrelated to the behaviour of the weather.

'I hope he ain't spoiling for a fight,' he said, 'him and whoever he brings with him.'

'Nope, he won't fight,' said Davey, 'he'll hold back until he gets wind of us and kill us all by shooting us in the back, or the back of the head, whichever's easiest.'

'And you led us here knowing what this ex-con was

capable of?' asked Ony, grimacing in the firelight.

'You weren't invited to a picnic,' said Davey, 'you knew this was risky.'

'Not in that way,' said Ony. 'I don't want my head blown off by some lunatic miscreant.'

'You know, I guess I feel the same way,' said Wattie. 'What about you, Buzz?' But their guide was looking particularly miserable.

'Truth to tell, if he knocked off my noggin he'd be doing me a favour,' he said. 'I ain't had a drink in days, and now I know the reason why I started. Still, I know you, Wattie, there's a good chance that you've brought something medicinal with you that we could crack open when we got what we wanted.' He stole a covert look at their packs, which were piled up together in a corner of the cave.

'I've got nothing,' said Wattie.

'But—' began Buzz.

'Nothing. I told you.' But his words sounded unconvincing, and every now and again their guide took what he thought was another hidden glance at their packs.

'The hell with it,' said Ony, a gambler to his very roots. 'You weren't appointed sheriff of Benson for nothing. Wattie, you're one of the best shots around. I take it you'll be keeping an eye out for that killer?'

'I sure will, and even though Davey's just laid it out for us, I suspected there was a reason for him coming out here despite it being the monsoon season. It also explains why our cowboy friend wants to push on despite his deep fear of the one liquid Buzz hates to drink.'

'At least the rains seem to be thinning a little,' said Davey.

'Can anyone else hear that noise?' asked Wattie. 'It's coming from the back of the cave.'

He picked up a branch that was sticking out of the campfire, and burning at one end only. Whistling softly under his breath, he walked towards the back of the cave. You couldn't be too careful. What if there was a nest of vipers that would slither across them when they were wrapped in and sleeping soundly in their bedrolls?

In the dim light from the torch, he looked at the wall at the back of the cave. He could detect a thick, cloying kind of smell, that was sweet and fetid at the same time. The ground beneath his boots was suddenly soft. Was there something crawling on the wall there? He thought it might be a rat at first, when he saw a dark form, a snout that turned towards him and a sudden glimpse of sharp white teeth. But the surface of the wall was too steep for any kind of rodent to cling on to. Then he noticed the dark membrane that joined the limbs, and the papery rustling intensified, only this time it was from above. He looked up and saw that the roof was much higher here than in the rest of the cave, and hanging from it were hundreds, perhaps thousands of these creatures. Galvanized by the light he had brought with him, they began to stir. Then they began to squeak, a noise that was made much louder by the echoing quality of the rock and the small space. Wattie stepped backwards, but it was too late, he was engulfed in a cloud of screeching black-winged bats that seemed set to choke the life out of him.

CHAPTER EIGHT

Even though they were in Oak Leaf Canyon, the three were still at odds with each other. The rains had started just as they were leaving the desert behind. They had to ford a fast-flowing river. Luckily, at the head of the valley, the water was not as deep as it was further on, so they were able to get across safely. Also luckily for them, Buzz had forgotten one salient fact about the side canyon where he and March had kept the cattle they had rustled from the surrounding countryside. The spur canyon contained a cave.

Ever a practical man, it was Hardin who spotted the shelter. Kurzwell had ordered them to dismount once they were at the furthest side of the canyon. In this area, on higher ground, the oak trees grew more thickly. His idea was simple enough.

'We'll shelter under those trees for a couple of days, and the canopy will keep us fairly dry. We'll get under canvas, it's the best thing to do.'

The trees were hard by the rustlers' pen. Kurzwell got his men to lead the animals to shelter, and even though he was soaked through, he went to look at the natural corral, bringing a reluctant Hardin with him.

'Look at this, I spotted it on our way here.' He picked up a bedraggled object. It was a skin sewn up with waxed thread, used for storing water, that the guide had dropped, unheeding when he had come to inspect the old gates.

'So what? It could have been here for years.'

'No, the material is new, and it's intact. The insects and the weather would have eaten away at the fabric long since. This container was dropped here just a short while ago.'

But Hardin was disregarding his master. He stepped forward, and on to the slightly sloping ground of the corral beyond where the gates would have been. 'Hey, lookee here, I think we got a solution to our problems, for now at least.'

He ran forward and tore at some overhanging green plants that had partially concealed the hole from view. It was another cave, by no means as spacious as the one annexed by Wattie and company, but Kurzwell and his men couldn't know that, and this was more than big enough for the three men.

'Yippee, we got us a shelter,' said Hardin. 'I'll go get Mule and we'll get our horses unloaded.' Just to make sure, he peered inside. Not being a wild mountain man, who would have known what might happen, he nearly lost his life.

There was a wild, screeching yowl, and a bolt of lightning with fur on came running at him, bearing more teeth and claws than was good enough for a man's peace of mind. Hampered by the slick he was wearing, Hardin tried to back away from the yellow screeching thing, and fell backwards heavily on the sward, which was knee high.

Kurzwell reached for his own gun, but as he pulled up the heavy fabric of his slick to fire on the creature, the bobcat – for that's what it was – gave another wild screech, leapt in his direction and then was gone in the general direction of the trees, lost to sight within seconds.

'Dammit,' said Hardin, struggling to get up again and adding a few choice words for good measure. Kurzwell helped him to his feet.

'You're all right,' he said, 'it was more scared of you than you were of it.'

'You could have fooled me,' snarled the former guard. 'What if it decides to come back?'

'We'll just have to take our chances. Now watch out it didn't have a mate.'

A cursory examination of the small cave showed that except for the heavy scent left behind by the animal, it contained nothing else. With the rain still falling heavily, they brought some of their supplies over and lit a fire at the cave entrance from some dry wood that they had been able to forage from the base of the oak trees. The rest of their goods were packed into a tent that they had erected between some trees that sat on higher ground. They brought the food in with them on the grounds that this was what was most likely to attract predators, and besides, they did not want it stolen.

As they sat there, they looked out at the gathering darkness with the rain still coming down. Perhaps the noisy downpour was not as hard as before, but the water fell with a dogged persistence that showed it was not going to go away soon. Kurzwell addressed his men as they were finishing their beans in molasses.

'Boys, I knew this wasn't going to be as easy as we thought. Now we know for certain there's others here after what we want, we'll have to hunt them down. There's no other way. Are you with me?'

With food inside them and warmth from the fire, the two men growled their assent. Kurzwell nodded.

'Then it's set. As soon as this downpour goes off we'll be on our way. Check your weapons, make sure they're working. We'll need them.'

Wattie screamed as a black cloud of bats engulfed him. He threw away his makeshift torch, which promptly went out, and threw his body to the ground. This was unfortunate from his point of view due to the softness underfoot being the guano produced by the bats over a good number of years. He expected that they would bury him now under their revolting furry bodies, bite into his exposed hands, neck and the back of his head. Ignoring the revolting substance beneath him, he prepared for the assault that would occur in a few seconds.

Nothing happened.

Now that the disturbing light had gone out, a host of the winged mammals decided that their aims had been achieved and fluttered back to the high part of the cave where they resumed their roost. Quite a few, though, decided that this was one intrusion too much and headed for the outside world, carefully avoiding the flickering fire.

Davey was still laughing out loud as he helped Wattie to his feet.

'Boy, you should have seen yourself dancing there fit to bust, I thought you was in some kind of jiggin' contest.' Davey could not still his laughter, but Ony was grinning from ear to ear, and even Buzz had temporarily forgotten his troubles, and he too laughed out loud at the sorry state of their companion.

'A few bats won't harm us,' said Davey. 'I've often slept in between the trees and seen 'em flying about. Fact is, you leave 'em alone, they'll leave you alone.'

'Goddamn critters,' muttered Wattie. He went out into the still pouring rain, stood under the shelter of the over-hang and wiped his jacket as best he could, scraping his boots on the bare rock.

His sorry accident seemed to have had the effect of breaking the ice, and for the rest of the evening, his companions regaled each other with tales of their exploits. Wattie recovered some of his aplomb and told stories of how he and Davey had become adroit at stealing horses in their homeland, and how Davey had nearly been strung up for the same offence. By mutual agreement they all agreed to turn in at the same time, after the rest laughed some more at Wattie, who was trying his best to pretend he was untroubled by their good-natured ribbing.

Wattie had difficulty getting to sleep. It was not that his bedroll was uncomfortable. In fact, in the old days, he had been used to sleeping under the stars, in situations far more gruelling than this, with cold air around him, and the possibility of freezing to death. When he at last fell into some kind of slumber, he had a dream in which the bats had returned, but this time they were the size of a man, and there was a big bat sliding across him to bite his throat. This was the point at which he awoke and sat bolt upright.

Davey and Ony were still fast asleep, and only the glowing embers of the fire spoke of its full-blown presence just a few hours before. It was in the faint light of the embers that Wattie was able to see a shadow the size of a man in the corner. That shadow was moving as stealthily as it could manage, and raking about in their packs. From the empty bedroll at his side, Wattie realized that he must be looking at Buzz.

Even as he watched, his eyes growing accustomed to this, the faintest of lights, Wattie saw that Buzz was withdrawing a container of some kind from the pile with a barely suppressed exclamation of glee at his find. Since Wattie had put the container there originally, he was unable to suppress a feeling of righteous indignation at the thought of what was being stolen.

He had planned for them to have a celebration if, and when, they found the gold ingots, which would involve them opening and tippling from a bottle of the finest Scotch then available in Benson. He had told no one about his cache, but obviously Buzz had long suspected that at least one person would be carrying the precious cargo.

With this in mind, Wattie rolled over so he did not alert his thieving companion, snaked across the ground like one of the serpents he so feared, and snatched the bottle from behind, plucking it from a hand that had not been expecting such a seizure.

Buzz gave a hoarse cry, turned and tried to get the

bottle back, but Wattie had the reflexes of one who has been refreshed by a nightmare and has been sharply awoken, while Buzz was sluggish due to lying awake to plan his coup. Wattie was about fifteen feet away from him before the thief managed to exclaim 'hey!' in a suitably indignant manner.

'Give it back,' added Buzz.

'Won't,' said Wattie.

'Goddamn, you'll give that to me,' said Buzz, an object appearing in his hand that even in the faint light from the remains of the fire Wattie was able to identify as his gun. 'You don't know what it's like.'

'What are you going to do?' asked Wattie, faintly astonished. 'Shoot me?'

This exchange had the effect of waking the other two. Ony leapt up and interposed his body between Buzz and Wattie.

'What the hell do you think you're doing?' he asked.

'I need that Scotch,' said Buzz. 'You don't understand, none of you.'

'Listen, I'm a saloon gambler,' said Ony, 'I have a glass at my side all the time. Know what's in it? Water, that's what, because you don't last in my game drunk. Can't you see, man, what it's done to you?'

'I'll give you ten seconds,' said Buzz, 'and if you don't hand it over, I'm gonna shoot you, Wattie, I swear I'll do it.'

'I guess you can have the booze then,' said Wattie in a resigned manner, walking forward slowly as he held out the bottle in the faint light. Buzz relaxed and reached out his left hand to take the precious container, when a figure erupted at his feet. It was Davey, who had been listening to the exchange and waiting for exactly the right time.

Most of Davey's scars had been gained when he was young and he had learned the value of biding his time. Like the others, he kept his gun to hand, and it took a bare second for him to extract it from its holster as he reared up and stood between Wattie and his nemesis.

'Drop it, cowboy,' he said, and the gun dropped from Buzz's hand, clattering to the stony ground, the noise echoing throughout the cave. 'Guess it's time we managed this business. You're dead meat.' There was a loud click that also reverberated throughout the cave as he cocked the firing pin. 'Say yer prayers, boy.'

'I wouldn't do that,' said a calm voice as the fourth occupant of the cave came back into play. It was Ony, and even in the dim light, his hands could be seen held out in conciliation.

'Why not? This here idjit's been moanin' and bringing the whole trip down since he started. I've seen it happen that a bullet in the head can do wonders for that.'

'Davey, you're angry,' said Wattie, also joining in the conversation. 'But the truth is, we need all the people we can get, and it ain't good to go around killing 'em when we might need an extra hand. Besides, you're forgetting that Charles here, if I give him his Sunday name, is kind of essential to our operation. He knows how to get to the rope bridge that marks our way.'

'Yep, he's right,' said Ony, 'you kill him, we might never get there.'

'It's true,' said Buzz eagerly, his attention away from

the drink now that he knew his skull might end up as the residence for a few lumps of lead. 'I know the way.'

Davey lowered his gun, kicking the other one away so that Buzz could not snatch it up.

'All right, but we tie this one up until the morning light so he doesn't cause us any more trouble.' Buzz did not like this, but he was hardly in a position to argue with his companions.

'Thanks for saving my life,' he said to his brother as the bonds were completed. Ony looked at him coldly.

'If it hadn't been for the fact you're useful to us I might've let him get on with it,' he said. 'You've become a burden to yourself as well as others.' He helped wrap his brother in the bedroll and Buzz turned his head away, saying nothing more.

Wattie concealed the bottle of Scotch by the simple method of keeping it by his side as he laid himself down to rest. Before doing so, he looked out to the inky blackness of the Arizona night.

'At least the rain's slowing down. If this keeps up, we can be on our way by early morning.' No one answered him.

Ony did not lie down immediately, he sat and stared at his inert brother for a long time, while Davey, having no conscience to speak of, had gone off to sleep almost immediately.

Wattie could feel a longing deep inside. Now he wanted to drink the precious fluid, but somehow he managed to restrain himself until he fell into a dark, dreamless sleep.

CHAPTER NINE

When the next day dawned, in a small cave a couple of miles away, three men awoke to the faint morning light that filtered in from above. The skies were starting to clear despite the rains of the night before, and even now the day looked as if it was going to be fairly warm. The three of them had dined on their supplies of beef jerky and beans warmed in a tin container over the fire the night before. Now they would have a breakfast of the same thing.

Because he had the most at stake, Kurzwell got out of the opening first and went to check the horses and mules. Fortunately they were all still there, still intact under the close branches of the trees, although the animals were looking as disgruntled as he felt. He went back to the cave and roused his companions.

'Come on, it's time to go.'

'What's the problem,' asked Mule sleepily, 'can't a man have an extra lie-in?' He looked at the aqua-blue of the sky, a nice change from the actual aqua that had been falling on them the day before.

'I'll tell you what the problem is,' said Kurzwell, 'if we just wait then they'll get ahead of us again. Davey Quinn and his companions'll be just as locked in by the weather as we were. If we set off now we can catch up with them.'

'I guess he's right,' joined in Hardin, siding once more with his bread-and-butter like any wise man would. 'Just give us a few minutes to get some eats and a smoke and we'll be with you, boss.'

Kurzwell had already done those things, so while they were performing their simple toilet, he was already carrying out their possessions and loading up the mules.

Once they were ready, they led their horses and mules out from under the dense trees. The river had burst its banks so much that they were plodding once more through what, to all intents and purposes, was a swamp. They tried to keep close to where the trees grew because the grass wasn't so high there, and the ground was less sodden, but even so they often had to move outwards to avoid stony protuberances. Another problem was the fact that the atmosphere was heating up rapidly as the day wore on. This might have seemed a pleasant problem compared with the day before when there had actually been a chill in the air, but it meant that all three were soon sweating copiously. They soon had to halt and drink large amounts of water. The weather was so draining that Mule once more began to dig in his heels.

'Why don't we just take our time? They'll be getting this as well. Looks to me as if we can rest at least an hour.'

'No point resting,' said Kurzwell in his quiet, reasonable voice. 'We've got to get on this or they'll reach the gold first.' He paused as if he had suddenly thought of an idea that would be useful to them. 'Wait a minute, maybe that's what we do. Why should we slog it out? We could let them get to the gold and fetch it out for us, that way we would avoid a lot of the effort in doing so.'

The other two men looked at him in a way that showed their lack of understanding.

'But what if they get into the canyon where it's hidden and decide to leave another way?' said Hardin. 'Then we'll still have to chase after their tails and they might get away if it's as treacherous as you make out.'

'That's the beauty of my scheme.' Kurzwell still looked as if he was thinking aloud. 'When we hid those ill-gotten gains, there was a reason for doing so in that precise location, we knew they would be hard to get to without help. They are going to find it easy enough to get in, but they'll have to climb to get out, and believe me, it won't be a shoo-in.'

'So what are you going to do?'

'I'll think of something.'

The canyon was far from smooth as they went further along and they came to the narrow area beside the bluff, fringed by the roaring river, beyond which was the cabin built by Buzz and March in their glory days. Kurzwell looked at this with a faint air of astonishment.

'Last time I was here this was still standing, it was a wreck but you could still shelter there. Looks as if the wind, rain, and river finally got their way.' It was a graphic reminder of what could happen to them if they slipped up regarding the elements.

They came to the place further on where the rocks were overhanging.

'When we were here, I was told by one of the robbers that there are caves in this area,' said Kurzwell. 'I didn't get to see them because we just rode straight through. It only took us a couple of days because the weather was good and we had plenty of supplies. It's amazing what you can do when you are able to ride lean and fast – and when the law's on your tail.'

'Why mention them then?' asked Hardin.

'Because we ain't out the monsoon season yet,' said Kurzwell, 'and it could well be that we need more and better shelter before this is all over. Look at that river, it's mighty dangerous. Tether up, boys, we've got some investigating to do.'

They tethered their animals where the trees grew in clumps. The soil was poorer here so there were not as many, but these were also protected by the overhanging ledges of rock.

'Mule, you keep back and protect the two of us with your Winchester,' said Kurzwell. 'Hardin, you come with me, get out your .44 and follow on.'

He himself had a smaller pistol, a Smith & Wesson, a .32. He liked the feel of it in his hand. It was small and lightweight and he could draw on a man in a brief second while the Colt, although devastating in that it could blow a big hole in a man, was not as accurate if you fired in a hurry, which was what they might have to do.

They found themselves on a kind of rocky path and saw the entrance to the big cave. Kurzwell held up his hand to halt his companion, but said nothing. They both waited. Around here the air was a little less muggy. They could hear the river flowing in the background and the gurgling sounds of water being absorbed by the thirsty ground. Unknown birds were singing lustily in the background and there was a kind of green scent in the air – the smell of lush vegetation taking advantage of the precious rains to grow at a tremendous rate. Those people who thought of the desert as being a dry, sandy hell-hole had never actually been there.

They waited for a few minutes with no sign of life, but Kurzwell, as observant as ever, had noticed horse droppings where his rivals had tethered their steeds, so he knew that they were close to their target and he was not about to risk his life if he did not need to. As they came closer, he noticed where the plants had been trodden down near the mouth of the cave and the large amount of brushwood that lay under the overhang. The brushwood had evidently been gathered for kindling.

Now his idea of letting them lead him to his prize had departed. If they could trap the enemy in one place then this was the time to get them. That enemy had moved their horses, but that might mean they had just shifted them further along into a more sheltered position and were still using the cave as their base.

Hardin moved forward, confident in his ability as a gunman, knowing that if he was going to take anyone by surprise he could shoot them down. Kurzwell, who was not as confident, held back. Hardin stopped, lowered his gun and gave a long low whistle.

'What?' Seeing that there was no danger, Kurzwell scrabbled forward and peered into the darkness of the cave.

*

Wattie was lying there as the dawn was still struggling to reach over the horizon. He had elected to put his bedroll near the dying fire on the grounds that the embers would keep him warm at least for half the night.

He had rolled onto his back and felt a raindrop on his forehead. This in itself was not unusual, he had often experienced dew falling on him when he was sleeping out in the open. There was, his slowly awaking brain told him, something wrong, because he wasn't outdoors. Wattie had trained himself from an early age to wake up in the face of the slightest danger, it was how he had survived his strenuous youth and it was how he intended to live into a slightly less active old age.

Wattie sat upright as he felt another, more distinctive splash on his forehead. He did not hesitate but roused the other three. Even Buzz had managed to fall into a deep sleep.

'Boys, get up, we got to get out of here. No time to explain, help me right now.'

'What the hell?'

Davey, being the eldest, seemed to value his slumber and Wattie had forgotten that Buzz was still tied up. Ony seemed to cotton on to the fact that there was something dire happening, even if it was not as obvious as a bear attack or a rattlesnake slithering amongst them. He ran with Wattie to the side of the cave and they literally began throwing their worldly goods out of the entrance.

Wattie, with a sudden attack of conscience, remembered that he had tied up Buzz, but the bonds had been tight, too tight for him to undo in the time left. He managed to bend over Buzz, unwrap him and half-pull him to his feet. Buzz, who seemed withdrawn and still half-asleep, stumbled out of the entrance and to the slope below, hands still tied behind his back.

In the meantime, Davey looked at all this activity open-mouthed.

'So there's a little drip in the place,' he said, 'you scared of water? This ain't some boarding house, it's a natural place, there's bound to be some kind of water in this mighty rough weather.

'Come out of there, Davey,' said Wattie, 'I think I know what's going on.' His words seemed to be backed up by the fact it was now, in effect, raining inside the cave that had been their home for the last day or so.

'All right, I'll join you yellow-bellies,' said Davey, strolling forward and over the lip of the cave. It was good that he did this, because the roof of the cave made a rumbling sound, and thousands of gallons of water took the easiest route and poured into the dark interior of what had been their makeshift home. If Davey had been under the spout where the most water fell, he would have been killed instantly. It was not just water, which has a considerable weight of its own, that came down, but also a rain of debris. As it was, he just barely dodged a large rock that nearly collided with his skull. He fell down as he struggled to get back towards his companions, and might have been sucked back into the dark pool inside the cave if it had not been for Wattie, who dodged into the interior, seized his old friend and pulled him out of the flooded mouth of the cave.

'You blamed idjit,' said Wattie, 'why can't you just come out when you're told? Look at me, I'm all wet now.'

Davey was the wettest man they had ever seen, standing there opening and closing his mouth like a particularly indignant fish.

'Well, there's nothing you can do now but just dry off,' said Wattie in a resigned voice. 'Come on, we'll move further along and I'll make us a fire and we can have some eats. You look as if you could do with a coffee, Davey.' He looked at Buzz. 'Ony, you can untie your brother now. Unless he wants to go skinny dipping, that drink's beyond him now.'

Later, when they had eaten and Davey had dried off somewhat, it was Ony who asked the obvious question.

'What the hell happened?'

'Well, the way I see it, there was a lot of water falling in a very short time. When water falls like that it has to go somewhere, and the rock around here ain't as solid as it looks, it has cracks and crevices all over the place. There must have been a hollow spot in the stone above the part of the cave where we was resting, and as the water leaked in from the rocky ridge above, it began to pool until the ceiling of the cave couldn't take the weight anymore.'

'That was a hell of a thing,' said Buzz. He put his coffee cup to his mouth, his hand was trembling. 'You should've just left me there. I ain't no use as a human being.'

'You said that right,' agreed Ony heartily. For a second Buzz looked as if he was going to throw the coffee in his brother's face, then he turned his visage downwards and said nothing.

'What is it with you two?' growled Davey, thankful that the attention was being diverted from his own predicament. He was of the opinion that the cave, of all things, had made a fool of him and Davey didn't like being a fool. He didn't like being laughed at, either, and when Wattie pulled him out of the wet space, Davey had looked more like a drowned rat than anything. He had seen their smirks and he was ready to teach the first man who took a rise out of him a severe lesson.

'Maybe you should ask Charlie boy here,' said Ony, looking at his brother. 'That said, he's doing a useful thing with his life now, ain't you, Charlie? Maybe this is just what you need, a jolt.'

'Well, the whiskey's gone,' said Wattie too brightly for some, 'unless, as I say, we've got an expert swimmer amongst us here.'

'Well, you won't be able to crawl into a bottle until we get back to Benson,' said Ony. 'Then you can dry up your innards and go to meet your maker as much as you want.'

'Ony,' said his friend, Wattie, 'this ain't being all that helpful.'

'What's the point of it all?' said Buzz, after brooding for a while. 'Seems to me there's no use going on, you might as well go find it for yourselves.'

Wattie shot a hostile look at Ony, the latter having an expression of pure annoyance on his face. This was another opportunity to pour salve on the wounds, but Ony did not seem all that keen to take up the challenge.

'Typical of you,' he said, 'leaving things at your butt, never finishing what you started. You've been the same all your life, why should you change now?'

'Well,' said Wattie judiciously, 'it looks as if you're managing to talk yourself out of a small fortune, Ony.'

'I oughter knock your heads together like two coconuts,' growled Davey. 'Make you see some kind of sense.'

'Is that what you think of me?' asked Buzz, still staring at the ground, although everyone knew whom he was addressing. 'I tried hard, mighty hard, when I was growing up. I left the city, went on the trails and rode herd with the best of them. Ask Davey, he knows me well. I worked real hard at moving the beeves out to market. I worked from here to Kansas and back. I was there when Benson became a rail town. I tried hard.'

'Not hard enough,' snapped Ony. 'You're just a useless pile of walking injun-fodder. I've seen better things than you crawling out from under rocks. You're worse than a heap of bull plop.'

Wattie had heard of people throwing up their hands in despair but had never actually seen this done, thinking it a convenient expression used in fiction, but now he did precisely that thing.

'Well, boys, we might as well pack our bags and head in the opposite direction because it sure looks as if we ain't going to be laying our hands on that gold.'

Davey, who was drying rapidly after his soaking jumped to his feet, and this time he actually drew on them.

'You two better settle your differences fast, because right now I don't see any reason for preserving either of your miserable carcasses. In fact, if anyone has a case for living it's Buzz because at least he knows where our gold is.'

Buzz still did not look up. He spoke in a low voice as if

addressing the ground, but in a low, grating tone that struck the others, even his combative brother.

'We was young, brought up in Tucson. It was a few years after the Civil War when the city was starting to prosper. We was both out to make money, then we came up against the Dalton gang. Ony was up for making money even then, doing jobs for the powers-that-be. He was only fourteen years old, and I was seventeen, when the Daltons, six of 'em, came for us. I was the only one with a gun at the time.'

'Go on,' said Ony in a harsh voice quite unlike his usual semi-cultured tones.

'It was in the main street and they was coming to teach us a lesson in public. I was young, I panicked, I gave my gun to Ony and I ran out of there. There's no excuse for what I did, I took the coward's way out.'

'You did,' said Ony. Then he paused. 'Luckily even then I could talk and talk well. I faced up to big Frank, the ringleader and I asked him why he was so mad at me and he told me it was because I was getting in the way of his business, which was to make money out of the city.'

'I went to rally some of our own friends,' said Buzz, 'that's all I can say. I genuinely thought I would be useless in a fight, and thought it was the best I could do. And I came back.'

'You came back when it was all over,' said Ony. 'You abandoned me.'

'And I felt like hell then, and I've felt like that ever since,' said Buzz.

'Then go to hell,' said Ony. They were facing each

87

other by then and something seemed to snap inside Buzz.

'Really? Is that what you think about me, you don't care a shit for how I feel?'

Buzz gave a sudden, inarticulate cry of rage and launched himself at his brother. It was still early on in the day and they were seated above where the water was still seeping into the earth below. The sudden attack had the effect of unbalancing both combatants and they rolled to the soaking grasses below. Davey started to run after them, but Wattie grabbed him by the arm.

'This is between the two of them, you must see that.'

Davey desisted and they watched as the two slugged it out. Ony was younger and seemingly fitter than his brother, but the easy life of the saloons had taken its toll, and he was not quite as fit as he appeared, while Buzz was still big and strong.

They punched out at each other in the waist-high grasses and Buzz connected with his brother's jaw. Ony gave an inarticulate cry and vanished into the tall growth around them. He did not reappear for a second, then Buzz was jerked forward as if by an invisible man. It was obvious that Ony had decided to stay low, and get his sibling that way. Buzz disappeared from sight; there was much muffled cursing and shouting as the pair fought it out, mostly hidden from sight in the undergrowth. The sounds continued for a minute or so, then there was a dead silence. No one reappeared.

'Well,' said Davey, breaking the spell, 'I guess one has choked the other. Wonder who's gonna survive?'

CHAPTER TEN

'I guess we don't have much of a problem with anyone lying in wait,' said Kurzwell. 'This damn place is full of water. I guess the rains must've leeched in because the rock here is kind of porous.'

'It could've been there for ages,' said Hardin.

'Not so, can't you *smell* the water? It's as fresh as the morning dew. Water that's been lying for a while has a sludgy stink, especially in a place like this, where the bugs and plants use it as their home. I think this is the result of our sodden downpour last night, and I still think it's where they were.' This was amply confirmed when they went further down the slopes and found evidence of a campfire a few hundred feet away on a rocky platform not too far from the base of the canyon. 'Yep, looks like they were almost caught last night and had to decamp here. Probably early in the morning. Seems to me we've almost caught up with them, wherever they are.'

'What're we going to do?' asked Hardin.

'I thought we were going to bump into our friends almost as soon as we came round that bluff, that's why we prepared for battle. Remember, we have the upper hand right now, they don't know we're on their tails. In fact, if it hadn't been for their cave flooding I reckon we might've bumped into them by now.'

'So what are we going to do?' repeated Hardin.

'Well, look, the trees're getting sparser already. I reckon we get the horses and mules, and take them to some kind of shelter close to the end of this canyon, leave the mules and take the horses only. If I'm right about this then they'll get across and go to the bridge as soon as they can. So we'll revert to plan A.'

'I guess so.' Hardin seemed mildly disappointed; Kurzwell gave him a sideways glance.

'Seems to me you were looking forward to a con-frontation, but trust me, it's better this way.'

The pair of them went back to where Mule was lying on a spur of rock overlooking the rocky slopes, his Winchester clutched in his hands, and with a look on his face that showed he too was a little sorry that they hadn't been able to dispose of the other party. With the rest out of the way, it would make their lives a little easier. They fetched the animals and rode on for at least another mile. In some ways the going was easier, because the grass that had grown so profusely before was giving way to more and more of the rocky base that lay underneath. The walls of the canyon widened out during this trip, but rose sheerly upwards so that they had to crane their necks to see the top. The route was far from straight as the curving of the river took them around several steep bends and back out again so that if they looked back, the original entrance was no longer visible.

The oaks, which needed a deeper soil, were now giving way to pinyon and fir trees. It was at a group of these that Kurzwell halted the party.

'What we'll do is get the mules under these ones. There's enough grass for feed and we can give them some oats and molasses,' said Kurzwell. 'We'll feed the horses too, then take them with us.' He was acutely aware that without the animals and their supplies, they would not survive the trip back to town. 'This is the time when we must proceed with caution,' said their leader, 'because if they become aware of us, they'll make sure that we're dead before they go for their prize.'

'They'll have to get us first,' said Mule with a wolfish grin. Kurzwell studied him for a full minute so that the thickset man began to look uncomfortable.

'Maybe you should just stay here and look after the animals. You might be too much trouble.'

'I'm not, honest, boss.'

'All right, but you'll do exactly what I say from now on.'

The three men advanced their horses forward but at a slow pace. One cause of their troubles was the rocky nature of the ground. As the steep walls of the canyon closed in again, the sound of the horses' hoofs began to echo off the walls. Kurzwell wasn't sure how far off from their target they were, but he did know if they went on like this they were going to be heard by their opponents. Finally he brought the small party to a halt.

'This seems further than when we first came here. I reckon we can't go on like this, though. We're going to have to go by foot. Then there's the river.'

'Seems to me you haven't thought this through,' said Hardin. 'you're leading us from one danger to another. We might have miles to go.'

'So you might,' said Kurzwell. 'What you've got to remember, John, is that when I came here with the Bronco Boys, that old gang of mine, a couple of years ago, that there river was nothing more than a muddy stream fed by a couple of natural springs. We took our horses straight over because they hardly sank into the mud. We never got wet the whole trip. This monsoon has changed everything.'

They got off their horses and prepared to move ahead. But this time the sky, which had been blue, was rapidly turning grey again. They had come to what looked like a rocky gate, with huge boulders and crags bordering the river on either side. The fact was that the canyon was getting ever deeper and that they were constantly going downwards. It was a wonder that anyone would want to come and live here in the first place, but the rains made it a very different place from usual. The rocks themselves were not a formidable barrier, it was just that the river here deepened and they had to go down the side of the fast-flowing water on foot. This was the barrier the others were facing. Kurzwell felt glad they did not have to get across.

'Once we get through this pass we'll hold up,' he said. 'We'll position ourselves and keep a look out for the enemy, that way they can do our job for us and we can get out of here.'

Now they were moving through an area of looming rock where the cliffs around them were not as high. They noticed the trees at the side of the canyon were thinning out again as the soil grew shallow. It was also an area where the sides of the canyon were more powdery, with plants growing out of them. Ahead they could see more large bluffs, spires of red sandstone, tall rocks and boulders of all shapes and sizes that had been carried down here by the force of the river in the past.

'We have to watch how close we get to those cliffs,' said Kurzwell in a voice that was little more than a whisper.

'And why would that be?' asked Hardin, who at least was taking some kind of interest in his surroundings.

'The walls are a mixture of rock and soil that has settled there over hundreds of years,' said Kurzwell, 'this is the worst rainy season that's been in this area for many years, far as I can tell. It makes the walls unstable. We'll find a place to stop and ambush Quinn that's a little safer.'

'I don't get this,' said Hardin. 'Why didn't we just wait back there where we would have been safer altogether?'

'Well, I've been thinking about that as well,' said Kurzwell. 'They ain't as stupid as you think. When men are carrying a couple of million dollars' worth of gold it makes 'em cautious. Most likely they would send a couple of scouts ahead to find the lie of the land before they brought up the gold, and there could have been a real good fight. This way we ambush them in a tight spot and get all the reward in one fell swoop.'

He could also have added that it was because he did not entirely trust his two aides, and that if they were closer to the entrance of Oak Leaf Canyon, they might well decide this would be a party of two rather than three, and since his companions were friends they might consider it wiser to get rid of the man who had financed this very trip.

They were still descending, with the rim-rock visible above them. There was a spot where the canyon opened up again, where the river was roaring downwards now and there was shelter beside a large butte. Now it was raining again. But Mule, who had keen eyes, looked ahead.

'There's something moving down there,' he said. So far they had seen very little in the way of wildlife except for the bobcat they had encountered on the trip. But this was an animal that slunk rapidly along the ground.

'It's a coyote,' said Mule.

He was sitting comfortably in his big Southern saddle. He instinctively disliked all wildlife and wanted it out of his way. Before his companions could stop him, he drew out his Winchester and fired at the animal, which saw the humans, did a complete about turn, and ran back down the valley. Mule had to fight to retain control of his horse, which bucked and whinnied as the noise of the shot reverberated in the air around.

'You blamed idiot.' Kurzwell twisted in his saddle. 'What the hell did you do that for?'

'It was coming towards us,' said Mule sullenly.

'So's the rain, but you don't shoot that. It was going to avoid us.' Kurzwell was so angry that he pulled out his pistol. 'You've messed this up for us all so I ought to shoot you in the head right now, except I'd be in danger of missing your brain.' Abruptly he put the pistol away.

Hardin pulled on the reins of his blue.

'Ride,' he said to his companions. 'Ride.' He did not waste any time but took his own advice.

The other two heard it then, a slow roar that was quite unlike that of the river flowing so quickly to the other side. The rocks and soil that made up the walls around here were so saturated from the long rain that they had become unstable. The one shot had been enough to trigger a chain reaction that had loosened some scree, leading to a larger mass becoming detached.

They were about to experience an avalanche.

Worse still was about to come. Mule, realizing what he had done, housed his Winchester in his saddle sheath, snatched at the reins of his mount, and kicked the animal in the sides. The horse, a big two-year-old called Brutus, was already startled by the noise of the shot and gave another whinny. He was in an unfamiliar environment and he too sensed that a violent change was in the air. He reared up, flailing his front hoofs, and Mule, who wasn't an experienced rider, was thrown to the ground. Brutus, now that he did not have to carry such a large weight, sprang forward and joined his fellow horses as they trotted away, all three unable to gallop because of the uneven, boulder-strewn ground.

Further down, up against the bluff, Kurzwell brought his horse to a halt, heeled him round and looked at the situation. Hardin too looked back just as Brutus arrived beside him, and they realized that they had lost their companion.

Mule was just beside an area where one of the trees, its roots dying years before, had tumbled to the ground and rested between some more rocks that stuck out from the ground like red fingers.

The sides of the canyon just beside where he stood gave a rumble like a giant grumbling in his sleep. Mule, who was still on the ground, rolled away but he was too late, a landslide of debris fell over him followed by descending rocks and loose stones. In a few seconds, he was buried from sight, and all the onlookers could do was watch in helpless bemusement.

CHAPTER ELEVEN

From within the long grass there was a shift and a loud groan. The brothers appeared, did not look at each other, but stumbled back to the ledge where the others waited.

'What happened?' asked Wattie.

'He got lucky,' said Ony.

'I don't want to talk about it,' said Buzz.

'He got his knee on my chest and had me pinned down. He could've bashed my head in – there's plenty of rocks amongst the grass, but he didn't,' said Ony. If there was one thing about him, it was the fact that he was prepared to face reality head on. 'I guess I should thank him for that at least.' He looked at his brother, who avoided his gaze.

'Now that you pantywaists have settled your differences, it's time for us to go,' put in Davey. 'It's getting hotter and we're losing time. If there's someone after us they'll be able to catch up fast.'

'Well, let's clear up here,' said Wattie, ever practical.

With the help of the others, he brushed away as many

signs of their fire as possible, then he cleared up any scraps of food, and threw them into the long grass. Then it was time to get on their horses again, now that they were starting the long, slow trek into the inner regions of the canyon system.

'We have to cross this river again at some point,' said Buzz as they rode on, volunteering his first information since his fight with Ony. 'The way we want to go is through a narrow pass, then a box canyon.'

'I know some fellas want to be left alone,' said Wattie, 'but this is verging on the ridiculous. Why would you want to settle in a place miles from any kind of civilization, and even build a smallholding there?'

'You're looking at unusual conditions,' said Buzz, 'there's normally water down here in the canyon, enough to survive anyways, but these flooded conditions are far from usual. When I was here I sometimes had to dig down to find the water that bubbled up from the aquifer, or even drink from the hot springs.'

Soon they were beyond the next bluff of rock, heading downwards at what seemed like an alarming rate. They were now much lower than when they had entered the canyon system, and the river was a roaring, leaping presence beside them. Since it was normally not as high or as wide as this, the part that was now riverbed also took in large rocky protrusions that would normally have been dry, so the waters were swirling, white rapids, broken by lethal projections. Wattie eyed these with some alarm.

'I guess we don't cross here,' he said as they rode onwards.

'No, but further down, the canyon evens out,' said

Buzz, 'that's where the river will be wider, and flatter, with fewer rapids and that's where we'll cross.'

'That was some rainfall,' said Ony. 'Worst I've ever seen in this region.'

'If it wasn't for the fact that I suspect we're being tracked, I would say we should hole up again, then we could wait a few days,' said Wattie, 'but it seems to me this Kurzwell is a pretty determined kind of fella, and if he's close behind he won't rest up until he has us in his sights.'

They came to the looming, yet visible cliffs to their left, the rim-rock decorated with sparse foliage and with plants growing here and there out of the rocky walls. There was one more steep descent and a large butte that almost took them to the edge of the water, but at this point, as Buzz had predicted, the land flattened out and it seemed that they were nearly at the deepest part of the canyon system.

This was where Buzz became useful. The river was abruptly channelled into a steep but narrow descent enclosed by an arch of rock. The landscape was divided into different approaches, all of which looked likely to take them to where they wanted. Buzz led them to one they would not have chosen. It was almost invisible, a tunnel of rock between high walls, and so narrow and fringed by plant life they would have missed it on their own. It was also the steepest descent they had made yet. They held back from talking as they descended, and it was clear now how Buzz and his companion had managed to get away from the ranchers for so long.

There was a 'ki-yikking,' sound in the distance that

alarmed Wattie and Ony.

'What the hell's that?' asked the sheriff.

'Coyotes,' said Buzz succinctly.

'Down this far?'

'There's deer as well, rabbits, rats, anything they can feed on. Rich pickings if you're a hunter.'

'Just as long as they keep away from us.'

They travelled on for another short distance until the canyon widened out again, with a good growth of pinyons, firs and low bushes to each side, some of them on the far bank, now covered in water halfway up their trunks where the river had spread out from what had once been a meandering stream.

Even though they had risen early in the morning – an act prompted by their involuntary shower – it was already getting towards late afternoon. Not that it was easy to tell down here where, to their left the cliffs rose a thousand feet or more, while to their right the land was more sloping but also bounded in by the high chain of the mountains.

'Look over there,' said Buzz, pointing across the water to what was really a steep hill more than a mountain. The lower slopes were faintly wooded, but higher up where the foliage fell away, they could see the object of their travels.

The rope bridge had been slung from this side of the canyon to the other. The ropes were not in the best of condition, and even from this angle – although it was hard to tell – some of the wooden steps looked as if they had fallen away.

'I don't get this,' said Wattie. 'Why did the settlers – I

presume there was a group of them – even need the bridge?'

'Simple enough,' said Buzz, 'if you go further down this valley and though a slot canyon, then climb up, you'll get to the same area, but it takes much longer. Same if you climb the hill there and go down the other side. The rope bridge cuts out a helluva lot of walking.'

'I see.' Wattie looked around the area through which they were passing. 'I'm guessing that they kept their cattle here, for grazing purposes, and would have taken the smaller domestic animals like hens, pigs and sheep across the bridge and into their sheltered smallhold-ings?'

'Yep, that's about it.' Buzz fell silent again, then spoke up. 'I guess I know the attraction of being here, no-one to trouble you, life on your own with only those you want to be bothered with.' He sighed. 'No booze to capture you.'

'Rubbish,' said Ony, 'you would've made your own.'

Up until now they had not encountered many animals, now they heard the noise of howling from the trees to their left, and a group of three coyotes broke from cover. Two of them fled downwards while the third came towards them, only veering off when it realized what it was looking at. These animals were used to the semi-arid conditions of the canyons, and had been badly disturbed by the change to their normal hunting grounds when the floods came. They would have gone hungry for the last couple of days, and that would have made them attack any one man on his own. The coyote that came towards them was a large dog, with a yellow coat, and a double set of fangs made for killing. It yowled at them as it passed by, and went higher up the slopes towards the butte around which they had just travelled and vanished from sight.

Davey snatched at his gun as the animal came near, but Wattie signalled for him to do nothing. Just as he had surmised, the animal – although desperate for food – was not stupid and avoided tackling them head on.

'I guess what's happened is that all the jack-rabbits have retreated deep into the ground,' said Wattie, 'and the deer will have headed for the high hills, and the more wooded parts of the canyon. As for any cattle that were here, who wants to put a bet on what happened to them in the last few years?'

'Their bones would've been picked clean by those fellas,' agreed Davey. He had been carefully avoiding a particular subject because it made him uncomfortable. This was a Davey they had never seen before. The bridge was in clear sight but he was spending his time talking about the animals that had gone. Wattie pin-pointed the reason why.

'There's no way out of it, Davey, we've got to find a way to get across this here stretch of water.'

Davey said nothing in response to this, but got his horse to walk up and down the area at a slow pace. The butte which they had circumvented so lately had a base that was far from even. A large, stony platform was the result, and this was a more interesting feature for Davey.

'Look across the other side,' he advised, 'see how the land rises in a slope there, from the water's edge? Iffen we get the horses to wade in they'll be over pretty quickly.' He did not look too enamoured at the thought. 'But look at the way the water's swirling, it's getting caught, and flung around that bend pretty quickly. If they're not strong enough to do this they'll get swept away.'

'The truth,' said Buzz, 'with our weight on them – 'specially yours, Wattie, the hosses will do fine, the only worry being if they slip on loose stones.'

'These old riverbeds're pretty smooth,' said Wattie, looking at the area being discussed with a keen eye. 'Davey, I think you're on to something, I reckon we can do this. The only thing is, once we're across there's a narrow strip of land in front of those trees before it all widens out again, that'll be tricky to get on to.'

'I've got an even better idea,' said Ony, 'we don't know for certain that anyone is close on our tails, why don't we wait a few hours and see if the water level goes down?'

This, of course, was the precise moment when the clouds came over and it started to rain again. 'But then again,' said Ony, 'there's no time like the present.'

As they sat there, with their hats on, the rain was quite a welcome relief from the heat of the day since it chilled the air, and it was not as heavy as that of the last few days. The monsoon weather, it seemed, was breaking a little, promising fairer times ahead.

Davey got off his horse, walked across to the stony platform and measured the distance from side to side with a gimlet eye.

'Yep,' he said, 'I reckon I can do this.'

'Reckon we all can,' said Wattie. 'Get back on your horse then, and we'll go. This rain's just going to get heavier and the horses will get more nervous.'

'Ain't doing this with a horse,' said Davey, in a quiet, stubborn manner that showed he was not going to be swayed by any arguments that might be put forward. 'I'm doing me a leap and gettin' over that way. You can lead ma horse, Wattie.'

'Davey,' said Wattie patiently, 'there's many reasons why you ain't going to make it that way, the best one being you'll never get the distance.'

'You say that,' replied his old friend, 'but remember when you and me was boys together, Wattie, and the time I jumped Sawbuck Creek to get away from that rancher?'

'I sure do,' said Wattie, 'but you've got to remember a few things. That creek wasn't a swirling river, and the second thing is that you're twenty years older.'

'There's a third thing,' added Ony. 'Davey, you're too much of a shorty to make that leap. Buzz here, he could do it in a second, even Wattie could have a fair try, but you can't get the height.'

'The hell with you all,' said Davey, now quivering with annoyance, 'I ain't going to get thrown by some stumble-footed nag, I'm doing this my way. Besides which.'

He had obviously been looking around on their way here, because he fetched a long piece of dead wood that had fallen from one of the beech trees. It was not exactly straight, but it was a pole of sorts. Wattie got off his horse to restrain the madman his friend had become, but before he could do anything, Davey ran across the stony platform, pushed down hard with the pole and launched his sparse body across the water.

All three onlookers were in awe as his body flew effort-

104

lessly through the air. Their warnings were going to be given the lie, and he was going to land safely on the other side. This would have been the case if it had not been for a monumental piece of bad luck. As Davey landed, he clutched at the nearest branch sticking out of a pine tree, his heels stuttering on the hard ground below. He failed to grab the branch and fell into the swirling pool of white water behind him.

In point of fact, all might have been well if Davey had kept his head. The area he had fallen into was close to the stony ground, so that if he had flung his body forward he would have had a fair chance of getting to a shallower part of the river. From there he could have got enough leverage to get back up to where he had landed. The trouble was, Davey, although he would never have admitted this to any of his companions, was simply afraid of the water. He gave a wordless scream, drifted onto his back, and flailed his arms and legs. This was a particularly ineffectual way of dealing with the tide of water that swept around the bend of the rock, gathered pace in a whirlpool, then joined the main body of the river.

Their companion managed to turn over and get onto his face, and this time he really did try to swim back towards them, a distance of mere yards at this point. He might well have succeeded too if he had been a heavier man, but Davey was far from large in build. His sparse frame had become even sparser in the desert climate as if all the juice had been sucked out of him, so that he simply did not have the heft and weight to battle against the confluence of the water as it pulled him away from the shore.

Another factor in his downfall that no-one could have taken into account was his clothing. Their trousers and jackets were deliberately large, and made of animal skins to act as insulation when they slept. Now the air trapped in his clothing buoyed him up and made him float. This might have seemed like a good thing, except for the fact that it prevented his feet from touching bottom, so that swimming was his only option, and swimming had been a failure.

Wattie flung off his own jacket, cast his hat down and began to wriggle out of his trousers. He was the most solidly built of the four, and he had the best chance of rescuing his old friend. He knew that if he kept on his own clothes he was risking floating too, and then they would both be swept away. It was Buzz who grabbed his companion and prevented him from going to the rescue.

'Don't be a durn fool,' he grated into Wattie's ear. 'Cain't you see he's done for?'

Wattie looked across with wide eyes, because he knew that Buzz was telling the truth. Davey had been caught, flung out like a cork across from the fast-flowing maelstrom at the opposite bank, and thrown into the main body of the water. Davey opened his mouth to shout for help, but this avenue too was cut off as he promptly swallowed a large amount of water, and only choked.

From this area of the canyon, to the narrow slot through which the river was being channelled, there was a distance of some 200 yards. The water was hitting the narrow channel where it turned into a weir over which the water rushed, going onwards at an even faster pace so

106

that Davey was carried away, his lean form gone seconds after he joined the main body of the river.

'Don't blame yourself,' said Ony, looking shaken by recent events. 'There's nothing you could have done.'

'How's about I could've got off my horse faster?' said Wattie, still numb with shock. 'He was killed by the very thing he feared most.'

'Well, what can we do?' said Buzz, who also looked shocked and a little bewildered by the loss of his old foreman.

'I'll tell you.' Ony was in a frame of mind to deliver a lecture. 'I'm sorry to lose Davey, he was a good guy to have in a tight spot, but we can't continue after this, after seeing what happened to him.' He looked to the trees over at the back of them. 'I suggest that we make camp over here, wait until this latest rain storm's gone down, watch for the level of water dropping, and then go across. That way we'll be in a lot less danger, and you said yourself, Buzz, that the water drops quick in these parts.'

'You heartless bastard,' said Buzz. 'Davey's gone and all you want to do is get the gold.'

'Hold up.' Wattie resumed his authority along with his clothing. 'We're all feeling bad right now, Buzz, but Ony's just being sensible. We'll just have to wait a little, that's all. Do you think Davey would've given up if it had been any of us?'

'I guess not,' mumbled Buzz. The three of them prepared to set up camp in the shelter of the trees, but as they started leading their horses to shelter there was a sound that would change everything.

A rifle shot rang through the air, muffled because it was some distance away, followed by the slow rumble of a distant avalanche.

CHAPTER TWELVE

'Come on,' said Kurzwell. 'Let's get away from here in case there's any more falling rock.' His companion turned with a face that had set like stone.

'I'm not leaving him. Dobbins is my friend, Henry, and you can do what you want with that knowledge.'

Of the items they had brought with them, when leaving the mules behind, the most useful were the short-handed shovels they were going to use to excavate the place where the gold was hidden. The shovels were tied to their packs with rawhide. Hardin rode his horse down to where the avalanche had come to rest, used his judge-ment as to where his friend might be buried, and began to dig furiously. Kurzwell waited for a minute or so more, then gave a resigned shrug, took up his own spade and began to dig too. It was back-breaking work, made worse by the fact that they had to pause now and then to make sure that no more of the loose scree was going to land on them, burying them in a similar fashion to their com-panion.

Fortunately the place where he had landed after

falling off his horse had been more than good for Dobbins, because the landslide had been largely halted by the fallen tree which had blocked the bigger rocks, allowing only the soil and smaller stones to cover him.

After a few minutes' work – and just when Kurzwell was about to proclaim that there was no point in continuing – Hardin's shovel found something soft. Hardin was wearing gloves – much needed when a man was handling leather reins all day – and he used his hands enclosed in these for protection like smaller shovels, pulling the earth away from his find. He had uncovered one of Dobbin's arms; without any hesitation he continued with the same process, up the arm, and saw the face of his old friend emerge from the soil. Kurzwell was now an onlooker as there was very little he could do to help without getting in the way of his companion.

'Looks as if he's dead,' said Kurzwell, studying the dirt-streaked face that Hardin uncovered. 'Still, you can't blame yourself for what happened.'

'Come on,' Hardin began to tug at the man's shoulders, 'give me a hand to get him out.'

Kurzwell obeyed, although it was clear from the look on his face that he thought there was little point in continuing with the process. They pulled the inert body away from the earth, rocks and trees over to the grass and laid him down.

'At least we can bury him,' said Hardin.

'He *was* buried,' pointed out Kurzwell.

'I'm talking about in a decent Christian manner,' said Hardin. Just after he spoke there was a grunt from the figure on the ground, a groan, and Mule tried to sit up.

He groaned again and his head fell back to the sward.

'You son of a gun,' said Hardin, 'I oughta kill you, you bastard, for the worry you've given me.' Dobbins gave another groan.

'Go ahead,' he replied in a guttaral voice, 'way I feel you'll be doing me a favour.'

Hardin fetched one of their water-skins, held the head of his companion up with one arm, and got him to drink a long draught of the plentiful liquid.

They managed to get him to sit up then, pulling him to the shelter of a large segmented rock with a tree at the back providing shelter from the falling rain.

'It's all right, we'll fix you a better hide than this,' said Hardin.

'Don't leave me,' said the stricken man.

'Can you walk?' enquired Kurzwell with deceptive gentleness.

'Not right now, one of my ankles is twisted and I've got at least one cracked rib,' groaned their companion. 'I ain't in no fit state to move.'

'Hmm, this sounds dire,' said their leader. 'I think Hardin's right, though. We can make a roof from some branches interwoven to keep out the rain, and we can put a blanket under you and one around you. That way you'll be all right until we come back.' Hardin agreed with this, while the injured man had no choice, and soon, using the rocks as a base, they had created a makeshift shelter to hold their companion.

'But you're still goin' to leave?'

'We have to, Mule,' said Hardin. 'Think of what that gold will do. We both have our lady friends to think of, and you have young'uns to think of too.'

But Mule just gazed at them both with sullen eyes.

'I'll die out here if you leave me.'

'No, you won't.' Kurzwell produced the Winchester '73 and laid it beside him. 'You're far enough away and so protected that if you shoot that thing, you should be OK. If any of those coyotes come near you, use that weapon, you're a good shot, you already showed that today.'

'How long'll you be away for?' asked Mule.

Hardin glanced at Kurzwell.

'That particular ball's in your court, Henry.'

'If we get across quickly we could be back within half a day. There's an outside chance it may take us twenty-four hours. Of course, it all depends on who we meet on the way there.'

'There you go, buddy, you might have to spend a few hours here in the dark, but you'll survive. I'll leave you a skin full of water and some food. You'll be fine.' He glanced around. Brutus was still nearby. 'I'll leave your horse so that if you recover a bit you can ride up and out of here, and wait further along where there's better shelter in the caves.'

'You're still leaving me alone.'

'Dobbins, we'll be back,' said Hardin. 'You should recover enough to get out of here and we'll all be rich.'

Mule grunted at this, but he did not protest any more as they went back to their horses.

'We'll follow on,' said Kurzwell, 'this bunch could have reached the gold by now. But there's only one way out of that valley, bar the slot at the far end, and that carries a

112

huge risk. They'll need to go by the bridge, it's by far the easiest route.'

'Then that's where we're going,' said Hardin.

'There may be some shooting involved.'

'Mood I'm in, I could do with some light relief,' said the ex-guard.

'Come on then, this rain is just going to get heavier.'

They made their way towards the rocky bluff that stood between them and their goal.

After what had happened to Davey, there was a certain amount of trepidation about what was going to occur when the rest attempted to cross the river. Their fears, as is often the case, turned out to be unfounded. The rain had grown heavier for a few minutes, then there had been bursts of lightning and the rumble of thunder. This was a false start, the storm had died down, the sky had cleared again, so the river had not become as swollen as they thought it might.

Wattie was the first to cross, and being a man who was more heavily built than the others and on a solid roan, he was soon at the opposite bank, urging his horse, Steel, onwards with a series of movements that came from using reins and feet well without spooking the animal. Once he was solidly on the opposite bank, the other horses, who were not stupid, saw that this could be done and followed suit, including Davey's own animal, who seemed determined not to be left behind. She was a smallish mare, called of all things, Daisy, who had been sold to her former master by a widow out in Benson, and she was a determined character.

The cause of their movement was simple enough. When they heard the sound of a rifle shot reverberating through the air, it was the first clear sign that they were not the only people in this system of canyons. Although the shot was followed by the sound of an avalanche, this was small comfort. They did not know how the party behind them was composed, there could have been six men on their trail, with dogs, for all they knew.

'I'm kind of thankful for that coyote,' said Wattie, 'or they would've snuck up on us unawares.'

By this time, all three of the party had crossed and were on the opposite bank from the wider part of the canyon. The reason trees grew so well down here was because water tended to find a level during the monsoon season. The roots of the trees went down deep in a place where crumbling soil from above had settled, forming enough earth for them to flourish away from the harshness of the desert. The party edged their way along the bank of the river, moving cautiously, because one slip would mean that they would fall in with their steeds, and possibly suffer from the same fate as their late companion. Once the way opened up again they were able to get to the foot of the hill, atop which was the rope bridge they were going to cross. The bridge was not visible from this angle.

'Look, see,' said Wattie as they stood at the wide sward beneath the hill, 'this ain't a natural circle, you can see where there was fencing at one time.'

'That's because the settlers here couldn't take their horses across to their homestead,' said Buzz, 'this would've been where the corral was situated.'

114

'Still doesn't make sense to me,' said Wattie. 'Why would anyone come here?'

'Times was mighty hard after the Civil War,' said Buzz, who seemed to know a little of the history of the place. 'March, my old boss, said it was veterans of that war who decided to light out on their own, get away from it all. They didn't do a bad job until the weather and the isolation got them. They didn't end their life here that long ago, considering we can still see signs that they had a corral in this area.'

The hill itself was not that steep. Some vegetation grew at the base, but like most of the rocky areas around here, it was bare at the top. No one said anything, but they got their weapons ready. There was a certain amount of urgency about the situation. They had done what they could with the horses, tethering them to the nearest mesquite trees, but their one aim was to get to their goal and none of them, understandably, wanted to be left behind.

'At least if they come after us now, we've got the advantage of being up high,' said Wattie.

He was putting a brave face on the experience. After climbing for about ten minutes, they were now well above the river, the foaming waters cutting a brown line through the landscape just before they descended to the weir below, the place where Davey's body would be floating right now. The thought of this was the only thing that spurred on the sheriff, for he had not been lying to them. Wattie had a problem, he hated heights. Already his skin was crawling at the thought of what they had to do, even though he could not voice his fears to his com-

115

panions. At least that might have been the case, if it had not been for the fact that now they were at the much vaunted bridge.

The problem was, it was a bridge no longer. The monsoon winds had obviously caught hold of the ropes at some point, twisting them about to the point where the steps had pulled away from the main body of the frame, so that most of them were hanging down in a useless manner. One of the ropes was completely free of steps. This was one bridge across which they would not be able to walk. Ony looked at their route with the eye of an experienced gambler.

'Would you say that we would have to climb down the other side of this hill, Wattie?'

'I sure would.' Wattie was not looking forward to that process, either, because the far side of the slope up which they had just walked, far from being an easy ramble, was steep, almost precipitous and about 200 feet off the ground, which was the reason for building the rope bridge in the first place.

'Then I guess we'll have to try another method. You've got some spare ties in the pack, haven't you, Wattie?'

'I have.' But Wattie felt a cold chill through his heart because even without being told what Ony was up to, he could feel a plan of action coming on. He handed over the lengths of rawhide which he fumbled from his pack, four of them, each a couple of feet long.

'Buzz,' said Ony, 'do that thing.' Without comment Buzz took one of the strips, tied the ends together, twisted it in the middle to form a loop at either side, then tied one of his bandanas around the middle.

'What the hell?' asked Wattie.

'Give him your bandana,' said Ony, 'and he'll do the same for you.' He looked at Wattie's face. 'When we was kids, we uster play a game where we strung a rope from one tree to another and slid down it, just using another bit of rope. But the heat uster make the fibres part, so Buzz uster cut bits of old cowhide, we would hold either side and then slide down that way.' There was a warmth in his voice as he talked about his brother that had not been there before.

'That was across a narrow creek,' said Wattie, 'this is a mite different, the valley is hundreds of feet away and a long way down.'

'The principle's the same,' said Ony, shrugging his shoulders. Even while they had been speaking, Buzz, who was glad to have a task to do, was finishing the third loop and started on the fourth.

'There's only three of us,' pointed out Wattie.

'Yep, but we'll have to send down at least one of our packs,' said Ony, 'we need access to food and shovels.'

Even as he spoke he took off his own pack, took out some of his clothing that he deemed unnecessary, and helped Wattie to repack using elements of all their goods. Two shovels and a hand pick were deemed good enough because one man could always have a rest while the other two were digging, and they could all cram into one tent if need be. One of the empty packs was folded and tied onto the full one for obvious reasons. The heavy weight was held up by Wattie and Ony as Buzz fastened the loop on either side.

'I've just had a thought,' said Wattie. 'what if the rope

117

breaks as the pack gets down there? What the hell do we do then?'

'There's another rope,' said Ony indifferently, 'and you're forgetting that we can climb down too, only it'll take us a lot longer. Let 'er rip.' The two men released their burden and stepped back. Ony did not seem to notice that Wattie was notably pale of face as one of the natives of the territory might have remarked.

The pack juddered at the top of the rope and came to a halt, anchored by its own weight. Again this was no problem for the boys from Texas. They grabbed the rope where it was anchored into the wood at the edge of the cliff, and gave it an almighty shake. The bag gave a shudder and started to slide along. As the descent became even more steep, it was carried along at a hearty rate of knots by its own weight, coming to a juddering halt as it reached the bottom.

Buzz and Ony gave each other looks of sheer delight then shook hands. They were united, for a time, by their need to reach their final destination.

'Time to go,' said Ony. 'I'll go first. I'll use my legs as an anchor and jam ma feet against the pack so I don't crash into it, then I'll lift maself and the pack off the rope and you two can follow.'

'Sure thing,' said Buzz, all ready to go. 'Do you want to go before me, Sheriff?'

'Don't bother.' Wattie shook his head. 'I ain't going.'

'What?' said Ony as he and his brother stared at their companion. 'What's the problem?'

'I'll tell you what the problem is,' said Wattie, 'there's no problem is what I've been thinking. You boys need

118

someone up here to look after the rest of our goods and keep an eye on the horses. You two are young and fit, I trust you to get the gold. I'll wait here all right.' There was a thin sheen of sweat on his forehead, uncalled for on a day when the sky was overcast and the winds were blowing one of the coolest breezes in the territory.

'That your final word?' asked Ony.

There was a look in his eye that Wattie did not like, and for the first time the sheriff saw the core of steel that was inside this young, almost angelic looking man. Inside the gambler, Ony, was the same determination that would have made the settlers come here, and he wasn't about to let his journey come to an end because of one man.

'It is,' said Wattie.

'Then the hell with you. Follow on, Buzz.' Ony put his length of rawhide to either side of the rope, held the loops, and slid casually down the rope. Since they were well over 200 feet above the ground at the starting point, this was quite a sight to see. He held on with his strong, young hands and lifted his feet, a cry of 'yee-haw' escaping from his lips as he slid quickly down. It was far from a cry of fear.

Ony lifted his legs as he slid away from his companions, and as promised he used them to help him slow down at the last, literal kick, when he halted against their pack.

The descent took a few seconds.

Buzz, with an indifference that was a treat to see, waited for Ony to unhook himself, and the pack from the rope, then followed his brother down in exactly the same manner. He too gave a wordless cry that might have been one of fear or pleasure, or even a mixture of both emotions. Only Wattie was left.

Wattie looked back down the hill they had just climbed, that had not been an easy journey, either. He hefted his six gun, his protection if the other party turned up.

There was, however, one major problem which, in his desire to stay away from the makeshift slide, that he had not taken into account. The high rock on which he stood was just that, a big rock. This area was completely bare with no place to hide. If any shooting was to start there was a fair chance that he would be picked off before he could deal with his enemies.

He looked back down to the foot of the valley where his friends were waving to him. They had the pack at their side and were shouting for him to join them. Wattie picked up the looped leather, looked long and fearfully at the descent. Then he put the loop down again and took out his gun.

Even as he gazed at the landscape of the valley beside the fast-flowing river, two horses emerged from the other side of the bluff beside the water. The horses were small and far away, and the men on them were even smaller. As a target they were hard for a man to hit even if he tried. The thought heartened him a little. They were well out of range. If that was the case then so was he.

The trouble was, that the river, which had been deep and foaming when they had crossed in the shallowest area, had started to diminish greatly in the time they had taken to get up here, find a way of getting down the broken bridge and into the valley. This meant that their pursuers would be able to cross more easily than had Wattie and his companions.

Another oversight was the fact that Wattie had put his rifle in his pack, thinking that he was going to join his companions below before his fears had overcome him. He heard a muffled shout from the new arrivals below, and saw that one of the men who had arrived was bearing a rifle of some kind. It was probably a Winchester, thought the sheriff, because that was the weapon most commonly used out here in the territories.

The problem, for Wattie, was the fact that a rifle changed everything since it had a much greater range, and was far more accurate than a Colt .45 or indeed all of the handguns available to the plainsman. It meant that when it came to those below, they could reach him while he couldn't reach them.

He did not have long to ponder on this inequality before there was another muffled shout from below that seemed to indicate that the two men wanted Wattie to lay down his weapons. Their voices rang off the surrounding cliffs in such a way it was hard to make out what they were saying. Wattie put his hands to his ears.

'Beg pardon?' he asked. This time he was able to hear the response.

'Lay down your weapon. We ain't here for a fight,' said the smaller of the two men.

'Can't oblige,' yelled Wattie, 'seeing as how you could draw a bead on me.'

He could see them waving to him from far below, and he waved back, teetering on the brow of the hill, then pulling away, glad that they could not see the rivulets of sweat that were running down his face, or feel the cramps in his stomach as he contemplated the height from which his friends had descended.

'Damn you, man,' said Wattie, talking to no-one but himself, 'get to it.'

He hoped that the rifle wasn't within range but this soon proved to be wishful thinking when a bullet zinged past his ear. Wattie was not a betting person, unlike his wife Cora, but he would have said that the odds of getting hit on a bare summit where there was a limited amount of movement would have been better than even. He fired a shot or two back, but in a desultory manner because he knew precisely what the effects would be: nothing, and he was right.

Another bullet kicked up the dust at his feet and yet another hit one of the wooden stanchions to which the rope bridge was affixed. This was a lot more serious, because although the rope was his last choice, it was also his one means of escape. At last Wattie faced up to the facts. If, by some miracle, he was able to evade their bullets, a possibility that looked increasingly unlikely, he would be able to hold them off. But that also meant they could keep taking pot-shots at him as long as they had bullets. Realistically he could charge down the steep hill towards them and shoot as he went, but that would mean risking a fall and he was not sure if he could prevent that from happening.

Wattie gave a deep sigh, picked up the rawhide loop Buzz had prepared for him, strung it over the rope of the former bridge, held on to either side and lunched his big body into the air. Another bullet rang past his head as he did so, almost hitting him. He still didn't know if he had made the right choice.

He held up his legs as he went, the leather cutting into his gloves and the rope sagging in an alarming manner as he picked up speed during his descent. He had his eyes fast closed and he stopped breathing during the trip. Both of these things were a mistake. From experience, Buzz and Ony had known to drop their legs and pull the loop in tight at the end of their trip to slow their descent. This did not happen to Wattie and he slammed into the wooden stanchion at the bottom at a speed that could easily have broken one or even both of his legs. Falling to the ground, he lay there groaning, winded and in pain.

His companions were not idle. They had heard the shots from above and they knew it would not be long before they were joined by their unwelcome visitors. Buzz went to one side and his brother to the other. Both were armed with Bowie knives that had been well-sharpened back home on whetstones. These knives were soon to prove their mettle as they sawed through the tough fibres of the rope that had once supported the bridge. Once the ropes parted, the remainder of the bridge was dragged away across the valley with a terrible clattering noise.

'Well,' said Wattie, forcing himself to sit up, 'that's that.'

CHAPTER THIRTEEN

When the two riders came to the widening of the canyon and saw a lone figure up beside the remains of the bridge, they reacted in two different ways. Kurzwell had it in his mind to talk to the man and get information, while Hardin pulled out his rifle to shoot him right away. After their short conversation and the disappearance of their prey, Kurzwell rounded on his companion.

'What the hell are you up to?'

'I thought that was the point. To get rid of them.'

'You don't do a frontal attack unless they're all in front of you.' The leader of the expedition shook his head. 'Well, judging by what he was up to, that bridge is in a mighty poor state compared with what it was last time I was here. Come on, let's go and have a look. And when we get to the top, crouch low and it might prevent what's left of your brains being spilled out of your fool head.'

They made their way across the waters at the narrow point used by the other party. Even in the last hour or so since the rest had crossed, the waters had started to ebb as the rainfall from the previous night, flowing from the

hills, and trapped down here, finally began to diminish. They were halfway up the hill, keeping low and taking it easy so that they would not be too fatigued when they got to the top, when there was a sudden clatter that cut through the air like the rattling of a thousand deadly snakes, as the bridge was finally freed from its bonds.

'We're finished,' said Hardin, his first reaction to the sound. 'Now we can't get down.'

'We can and we will get down there,' said Kurzwell, coming to a halt, 'there's two million reasons why we're going to do so.' Hardin turned and began to go back down the slope.

'Where the hell are you going?'

'Not much point us completing this side of the trip, is there?'

'Come with me, I'm going to show you the lie of the land. Just watch out for stray bullets, because they'll be jumpy.'

The pair finally managed to make it to the summit. They laid down beside a rise to the left of where the bridge had been and inched cautiously towards the edge. Henry had been here before, so what he saw held no surprises for him, but his companion, who expected just to see another bare canyon, was astonished by what he saw. In the valley below the mound where the rope bridge would have halted, was habitation that could easily have housed a family of four or more. The structure, built as it was from a mixture of adobe and stone, was still fairly solid. To the right of this, marked out by a mixture of boulders and pebbles, the remains could be seen of what had been fields of corn and beans.

At the bottom of the valley was a tributary of the main river where the water would have come from to serve their needs. Also in this area were the broken pens that would have once contained pigs and sheep. There was plenty of vegetation, although the grass in the valley was sparse because the sun did not shine as brightly here due to the towering cliffs that surrounded the entire area. Hardin was mute with surprise.

'Didn't expect that, huh? That's why we were able to get away for a whiles, take some of the goods and get back to town.' Said Kurzwell.

'But if you had this, and were in a mind to stay, why would you leave?'

'A little thing called drought. There's not much of a living down here when the water dries up. It was the same for the settlers. Oh, they may have stuck it out for a while, but when there's two, three years of drought, you just can't survive here long-term. It was bad luck too. There's native buildings in these canyons, Pueblo injuns, who lived around here for hundreds of years, this bunch just happened to have the bad luck of hitting three drought years in a row and it drove them back to so-called civilization.'

'You seem to know a lot about it.'

'I'm going to tell you something.' Kurzwell rubbed his jaw. 'Reason I know all that is cos this was my home once. I was a child of the settlers. I helped my ma, pa, and grandparents build that very bridge that they've just destroyed. Ah, the hell with it.'

'I figured you for a dark horse, Kurzwell.' Hardin narrowed his eyes. 'Any other surprises, like you're really in cahoots with that other bunch?'

'See reason, John boy.'

'Explains a lot about you, why you're such a lone wolf.'

Hardin scanned the valley but he could see no other sign of life. It seemed that the others had made sure that they were not easy targets. There was no sign of them in the house, and any sounds they were making were lost several hundred feet below.

Kurzwell looked at the rope to his left that had once held up the bridge and gave a satisfied nod.

'How are you for heights?' he asked his companion.

'Never really thought about it,' said Hardin.

'Well, think about it now, because when it's getting on for dawn, you and I are going to make our move.'

They went back down the hill and pitched their tent on this same side of the river. It was doubtful if they were going to be attacked from the other travellers. Hardin managed to kill a jack-rabbit with his knife, and they cooked and ate this with beans in molasses while the fire flickered and danced in front of them as the darkness began to creep in.

'You keep guard, Wattie,' said Ony briskly, 'and we'll look for the cache.'

'I don't think so,' said Wattie amiably, looking a little less shaken and still aching although he would never have admitted this to either of them. 'Buzz, you can do the honours if you don't mind.'

'Why?'

'Because you're brothers, that's why. Now I'm not a mistrustful man, but I've been hurt, near drowned and

127

just plain rattled by what's happened. You might just be ready to cut loose if you find that gold and leave an old friend out of the deal.'

'All right,' said Ony, 'all three of us will look for the gold then. We'll just have to be on our guard for anyone taking pot-shots at us.'

'Maybe it'll work out better that way,' said Buzz, speaking for the first time since his joyful slide into the valley. 'After all, if we're lookin', they'll have to keep tracking us down from above, and that ain't as easy as it looks.'

'They might come down the ropes that are still dangling there,' pointed out Ony.

'They might,' agreed Wattie, 'but it would be a mighty difficult descent, and we could pick 'em off because we would see them coming. I say we get looking and worry about them when we need to. So, Buzz, lead us to where the gold's being kept.'

'I don't know,' said that gentleman. 'How would I know that?'

Wattie stared at him.

'You're our guide.'

'But think about it, all I knew was how to get to the bridge, or in this case what remains of it. I was hiding in the valley years ago, long before the robbery happened, and may I say just about the time the settlers had been driven out of here by drought. Me an' old March avoided coming down here because we decided that if the ranchers caught us we would be trapped.'

'You know, I never thought of that,' said Wattie. 'You were just a guide to get us here. Durn it, I was so caught up in what we were doing I forgot poor old Davey started the whole thing.'

By almost unanimous agreement the three decided that the best place to start was the homestead. It was a fairly robust building, but because of the fact that the higher walls were made of adobe, it had started to crumble, and some of the interior walls had fallen away, even so it was soon obvious that there was nothing hidden under the rubble and even the lower floors looked undisturbed.

Wattie gave the matter some thought while they were looking, and came to the conclusion that another, less obvious place would be where the gold was hidden.

'If it was me I wouldn't bury it in the ground,' he told the others, 'because the earth is prone to shifting due to floods and other disturbances, I would've put it somewhere else.'

'Like where?' asked Ony.

'If it was me, again, I would find some natural opening in the side of the rockface, one that was fairly solid, hide the gold inside, and jam it to the gunnels with stones and earth,' said Wattie. 'Call me simple, but that's the way I'd do it.'

This gave their search a new lease of life and they left the old building to go into the valley itself. They started on the far side away from the ruin, where the ropes and the remains of the weathered wooden steps still hung down, rattling occasionally in the winds that soughed through the valley from above. Now that they were on the far side of the valley, they did not have to worry about being shot at. The area itself was rather like a misshapen V with the wide end as their starting point, the narrow part being where the valley descended into the slot canyon beyond. By this time it was growing dark, because even at the first hint of twilight from above, the shadows down here grew deep, and Wattie was anxious to get on before true darkness fell. They walked steadily along, looking for breaks and occlusions in the wall of rock before them.

As usual it was the sharp-eyed Ony who spotted what they were looking for.

'Come have look-see at this, you guys.' He pointed to a well-covered area of the rocky wall that had evidently been filled in, and then smoothed over with a mixture of earth and clay. If they had not been looking for such a feature it would have been easy to miss, since it blended in so well with the surrounding area. Luckily they had the good sense to bring their shovels with them as well as the hand-pick that Wattie had thoughtfully packed along with everything else.

'This must have been where they put their ill-gotten gains,' said the sheriff. 'They'll soon be our ill-gotten gains.'

'What do you mean by that?' asked Ony suspiciously.

'I mean that now we're here we'll get what we need,' said Wattie.'It just sits a little uneasy with me, that's all.'

'We've worked hard for this,' pointed out Ony, 'and we're about to work a lot harder.'

'Gaining from the misfortune of others. Oh, the hell with it. Looks as if they packed it real tight,' said Wattie thoughtfully. 'I don't think we'll be able to get much done before dark.'

'Can't hang about,' said Buzz, 'not with them others

on our tracks. I say we make a start and get as much done as we can, then start again at dawn.' He stood up in the twilight and there was an aura of strength about him that had not been there before. His hands had stopped trembling and his eyes were bright. He looked more like his brother than the shambling wreck who had started the trip with them.

Their target was only a few feet across so all three fell to it with a will. Wattie was the biggest of the three and although his pick was small as befitted something that had to fit his pack, he cleared away the packed stones and earth with a will. The three of them soon began to clear a sizeable gap, but the packed stones seemed to go back further than needed.

'They really shut this away,' said Wattie, stopping and panting. 'Look around us, the light's nearly gone, we'll finish this during the day. We'll be up first thing.' There was nothing for the other two to do but agree with him.

Kurzwell began to move to the other side of the hill upon which they stood, keeping well back so that he could not be seen. He signalled for his companion to come with him. The time was early dawn but they had both been up since just before the light had started to creep over the horizon. They had already discussed the matter before taking the hard climb that had brought them to the summit.

'The trouble with those cowboys is that they don't see what's right in front of their noses. If they took the time to look around they would find other ways of getting down, and back up. The bridge was built as an exercise in engineering, and as a way of passing the time, of which we had plenty away from the towns and cities. But how do you think we got up and down before it was there?'

Now he led his companion to a slope to the far left of where the bridge had been situated. The hill dipped downwards again, and in a gash in the rock they found a short passage concealed by the stony walls. They now found themselves on a pathway, if that was what they could call the steep descent so faintly marked out before them.

'See, this is how we used to get to our home,' whispered Kurwell. 'It's a split in the volcanic rock that goes all the way to the ground. I'll lead the way and you follow. Don't worry, it's not as steep as it looks.'

He began to walk at an easy pace, followed by his younger, larger companion. They were both wrapped in warm clothing against the chill of the early morning air, and they both carried guns in their belts, and shovels on their backs, while Hardin had his Winchester slung across his shoulders for quick use.

Kurzwell was quick-footed in his descent, the pathways of his youth familiar to him, but Hardin was much slower, so that the leader had to stop and wait for him to catch up. It was not an easy descent because the path turned around some extremely steep bends, and it would have been easy to lose footing on these. Luckily one or two tough bushes grew out of the earthy walls and Hardin was able to use these for leverage.

'The path comes out at the base of the hill, but it's fringed by plants,' said Kurzwell in the same low voice, 'that's why they haven't seen the gap, and remember, if they do find it, to them it just looks like a break in the rock, and they don't know what they're looking for.'

They fell into almost complete silence now except for the stuttering of their feet on the stony path. As they came closer to the valley they could plainly hear the sound of men digging. Hardin smiled with a kind of grim satisfaction and began to ready his rifle.

'What are you doing?' whispered Kurzwell.

'We'll gun them down before they know we're here,' said Hardin.

'I don't think so.'

'What?'

'We'll need somebody to carry that gold for us. In case you didn't know, it's pretty heavy, and we don't have an easy way out now.'

They would have slaves to follow their commands.

Hardin gazed at his leader in the gathering dawn and gave a smile of sheer contentment.

CHAPTER
FOURTEEN

At first light the three men went across the valley and resumed their work. They had turned in early the night before, and slept two at a time with the third standing guard. They had dined on cold beef jerky with cold beans in molasses, electing not to light a fire which might attract shots from above.

Now, in the gathering light they dug into what had become a small cavern in the side of the valley. Wattie could picture what had happened. The robbers, fearing the full force of the law, had either used a natural feature, or had blasted the hole with dynamite. They had hidden the gold here, departing together – in case of betrayal by one or other of the gang – leaving behind the nest-egg that they would dig up in six months, a year or even two years later when all the fuss had died down.

Ony, who was the youngest and the smallest, did the final dig as befitted the one who had financed the expedition. The other two leaned in with him, both forgetting where they were in the lust for the hidden treasure that had taken hold of them. Ony threw down his short-handed shovel, hooked at something and pulled it away from the remaining earth. A canvas bag was pulled out into the light of day as he strained to shift it towards him, Buzz helped him pull it out into the open. Wattie could see that it had been crudely corded together at the top with lengths of twine. He cut the twine impatiently with his Bowie knife and the top of the bag gaped open.

All the hardships fell away, even the loss of their companion. Davey was the least of their worries now as they gazed down at the gold ingots that met their eyes as the bag fell open in the early morning light. None of them had seen anything as beautiful in their lives before. The men who had been bringing this wonderful metal to the US had paid with their lives, yet it was easy to see why this precious metal was so valuable that explorers had conquered whole nations seeking its lustre. The ingots were small, and weighed twenty ounces each. Each one worth a great deal of money. Wattie picked one up, and even in the early dawn within the valley it seemed to glow with an inner light.

'We'd best get to work,' he said. 'The first thing is, I'd better get back on guard while we divide the gold between three packs.' He put back the ingot and stood up.

Ony and Buzz were still looking at their find with wide eyes, no longer the tough men they had seemed to be.

There was a click from behind the three of them, the sound of a rifle being cocked.

'Hands up, boys,' said Kurzwell, 'and thanks, you did a good job.'

Three men walked through the valley towards the slot canyon, each of them carrying a bag laden with gold. Even Kurzwell had deemed the upwards path too steep and too risky for such a venture. He did not reveal the truth – that the ascent was riddled with so many bends that it would be easy to lose sight of the man in front and so risk a rebellion that might overthrow his captors.

The moment they were confronted, Buzz had started forward with a strange look on his face. It was as if he was taking their situation personally, or maybe it was because the lustre of the precious metal had shifted some kind of gear inside his head. He had only stopped short when a bullet ricocheted off the ground at his feet, loosed off by Kurzwell.

'Try that one again and we'll be leaving here one man short,' drawled Kurzwell.

'Get back,' said Wattie, 'he means it.'

'I'll see you in hell,' said Buzz, a confident prediction that drew smiles from their would-be captors. But he did not risk being shot again.

The two late arrivals could have shot down their enemy, but this was not the way that Henry worked. If he killed them and left, the two remaining men would have the duty of hauling the gold out of there, and there was no point in handling such a heavy burden when there was someone who could do it for them.

Stripped of their weapons, which Hardin put in his pack as they might be useful later on, the three were each given a load, and made to walk towards the foot of the valley, where it sloped into the slot canyon, a narrow aperture that descended downwards.

'This way it's easier for us all,' said Kurzwell, 'we'll all get back to the side of the river and our horses, then we'll decide what to do.'

Wattie said nothing but there was a look in his eyes that said he was not about to let them fool him for a second.

'Well, Henry, how do you expect us to get out of here when the river's flowing so fast?'

'Wait, how do you know my name?'

'I know of you, and I know what your gang did, slaughtering those men on that train.'

'I wasn't connected with that,' said Kurzwell.

'But you were in the area, and you knew this place better than anyone. Remember, I'm a sheriff, I look out for people like you.'

'Let's gun this one down,' said Hardin, 'he's a bit too mealy-mouthed.'

'No, wait,' said Kurzwell, 'he's still useful to us.' He turned to Wattie. 'As for the fact we'll be trapped by the water, you're wrong. With no natural spring to feed the river, it's already tailing off. The foot of this canyon will take us round to where we need to go, then back up the river bank.'

The canyon into which they had entered was just wide enough for two men to walk abreast of each other. Kurzwell was at the back with Wattie, while up front Hardin supervised the brothers. He kept a wary eye on Buzz who was still a little skittish and defiant, and being an experienced prison guard, he knew precisely the signs to look for when a prisoner was about to become rebellious. He was not about to give the man a chance to do so.

There was water beneath their feet as they walked, and this deepened to a couple of inches as they descended further into the twilight of the slot. There was a green smell down here where thousands of minute plants festered in the semi-darkness and the sky was a line of azure blue over a thousand feet above.

Wattie, who was sensitive to such things, thought he heard a noise like someone, or something moving in the shadows ahead of them. It could have been anything from a deer to a beaver – although such wildlife rarely came down this far, but it prompted him to speak again.

'So, Henry, what are you going to do with us? Don't you think it would be in our mutual interests for you and your friend, who I heard you call 'John' to put down your weapons and share this trip with us as companions?' He spoke loudly so that his friends could hear.

'That might be a possibility,' said Kurzwell. 'We didn't come all this way to fight and get killed, eh, Johnny?' But Hardin just grunted. Wattie sensed that he was going to be a hard nut to crack.

The canyon rounded a bend, coming literally to rock bottom before widening out into the space where the river poured into an opening that took it underground. The place was roomy, and littered with huge boulders that had been brought down here in the past by many a deluge far worse than the one they had experienced. Now they had to turn and go back up towards the box canyon where their horses had been tethered.

'Hope you didn't harm our mounts,' said Wattie.

'Why should we?' replied Kurzwell with a wide open smile. 'They'll be useful for when we get out of here and back to the desert.' The obvious follow-up question to this was what was going to happen to the men they had captured, but Wattie had a feeling that he didn't really want to know the answer to that one. All they could do was try and make a break for it, they just needed the right chance.

From a place of concealment not far away, a shot rang out, the sound echoing around them in the more open space into which they had emerged. Hardin, who was used to reacting quickly in his job, whirled around to face the sound. Another shot rang out and suddenly he was clutching in agony at a wounded arm, while his rifle lay unheeded at his feet since he had dropped it in his pain. Yet another shot whistled close enough to Kurzwell's head for him to duck down, with Wattie bringing his foot up and kicking the weapon out of his former captor's hand.

Buzz did not wait for instructions. Dropping his bag of gold, he picked up the fallen rifle with a speed that had to be seen to be believed and pointed the barrel at the head of the wounded man.

As he did so, Kurzwell dived for his pistol, which had clattered off the rocks. But he had a fine head of brown hair, which was his undoing, since it was this that Wattie grabbed on to as he dragged his opponent away from where the weapon lay.

As the shots rang out Buzz wasted no time. He jumped forward and swung a fist that connected with the jaw of

139

the wounded man. This would have felled Hardin, but he was a man who was used to dealing with prisoners, some of whom had been extremely violent men. Acting by instinct more than thought, the former guard stepped back and the blow merely brushed his chin. Also acting on the same instinct, Hardin put out his right foot – a ploy he had often used in the past, and the momentum of his attack meant that Buzz tripped over the extended limb and fell forward on the uneven ground.

Hardin gave a snarl of pure hatred and he was about to stamp on the head of his enemy with heavy boots, a move that would have hurt his opponent badly, when he heard a click and felt an iron muzzle at the base of his skull.

'Give it a rest, bastard, unless you want your brains blasted out of that thick skull of yours.'

He had forgotten about Ony.

In the meantime, Wattie was still battling with Kurzwell for possession of the Colt .45. It was a large weapon and not easy to grab hold of if someone was trying to prevent you from doing so. Kurzwell had turned when Wattie grabbed him. He too had a disregard for the courtesies of the fight, and he kicked Wattie on the left knee with the point of his boot. This had the effect of knocking Wattie to one side, taking him away from where the gun lay. It also meant that Kurzwell was closer to the weapon.

Wattie was not finished, and as he fell he grasped at Kurzwell's jacket and pulled that person down too. Because the sheriff was a larger build, the weight he brought to the contest unseated his opponent.

There had been no more shots from behind the boulders, either because the unknown gunman had run out of bullets or because he was afraid of hitting the former prisoners.

Wattie knew that if Kurzwell got hold of the Colt he would shoot down Ony, who was concentrating his attention on Hardin. Ony knew that the big man was a threat, and that even wounded, he was a dangerous opponent who was more than capable of surprising them all.

Now Wattie, more by luck than judgement, had managed to pull his opponent down too. This left them more than equal because Wattie had the longer reach. He grasped the butt of the gun, and finally had it within his grasp. He rolled over and started rising to his feet. This was a good move because Kurzwell had picked up a large piece of stone, and pounded it to the ground where Wattie's head had been precisely one second before.

'Cease and desist,' said Wattie grimly, but with an air of triumph, levelling the gun at his enemy, and Kurzwell, who was still on his knees, gave a groan of despair.

Their packs had been forgotten during the fight, but now Buzz limped over and made sure they were in the one place. They had worked hard to get this far and they weren't about to give up on their mission.

'What now?' asked Buzz, turning to Wattie as a solid presence.

'We take off their bullet belts and stow them away. Then I guess we don't move off until we find out what's going on,' said Wattie.

But he did not have to wait long for an answer. There was a dry cough and a series of echoing footfalls between

141

the boulders where the shots had come from. A scowling figure in black emerged and came straight towards them.

'How do?' asked Davey.

CHAPTER FIFTEEN

'I,' said Wattie, 'would like to know how the hell you survived.'

It was barely half an hour later, and they had not yet shifted from the spot. Their time had been spent greeting Davey in astonishment, then turning their attention to the prisoners.

'I guess we ought to shoot them in the head,' said Wattie. 'It would certainly solve a lot of our problems.'

'Let me blow his head right off his shoulders,' said Ony, speaking of Hardin.

'Don't rightly know if that's the right thing to do after all,' said Wattie, 'given that we set off to get this gold, not to go around killing people.'

'They were going to kill us. Weren't you?' said Ony, prodding Hardin viciously in the back. 'You were going to get us to the horses, load the gold into their saddle bags, shoot us and throw us into the river.'

'The hell with you.' Hardin's face twisted into a grimace of defiance, then his countenance took on a look of youthful surprise and he fell to the ground, unconscious.

'I've seen this before, said Wattie, 'it's the shock of being shot, and the blood loss.'

He used a strip of cloth from the man's own shirt, and bound the wound. Before doing this, he handed the gun over to Buzz, who kept a careful eye on Kurzwell. Once the wound was bound and some water splashed on his face, Hardin recovered, stumbling to his feet. He was dazed and confused now, and remained subdued. It was at this point that Wattie asked his famous question of Davey, who had stood by the whole time they were dealing with the prisoner, never taking the scowl off his features.

'I'll tell you what happened. After that there water swept me away, I saw my life flash before my eyes. Didn't take long, because it was mostly a life of herding beeves, hard drinking, womanizing, and setting up failed ventures. I prepared to meet my maker.'

'Didn't know you was religious, Davey,' said Ony.

'In that situation any piety you had as a boy comes back mighty quick,' said Davey. 'I said more prayers in three minutes than in the last thirty years.' He shook his head at the thought. 'The water carried me over that hump in the land there, and then you know what? It broadened out and I wasn't being swept forward at the same rate no more. I was half-dead then, as you can guess, but before I got swept underground I was jammed up against one of them boulders over there. Half-dead or not, I managed to get to the shore then I passed out. Luckily for me the warmth had reached down here,' said Davey. 'I lay for a long time and dried off. I always carry some basics with me, wrapped in oilskin, matches and the

144

like. Happily they had survived the rush down into this place. There was plenty of brushwood, too, that had been swept down here in the past, so I was able to make a low fire and survive here. Even my gun, sealed in a leather holster, was pretty intact.'

'Why didn't you try and alert us?' asked Wattie. 'Even if we couldn't have got to you because of how fast the water was, we would at least have known you were here.'

'I lay here for the longest while,' said Davey, 'it was hours before I was able to do anything, and the night had come on before I was properly able to move. So I figured there was nothing else to do but hunker down and wait. In fact, it's now that the water's mostly gone that I was going to try and walk back up into the broad canyon, when really it would have made more sense to take the other route.'

'I guess we wouldn't have heard you,' said Wattie, 'and after the avalanche, I suppose you didn't want to take the chance of another rock fall if you made too much noise.'

'Yep, that's about it.' Davey looked sharply at their prisoners who were not saying anything. Kurzwell was looking bland, while Hardin was white-faced and did not look all that well. He was still in shock from having been wounded. 'Guess it's time we got out of here, but first. . . .' He opened one of the packs containing what they had come here for, and he stared at the gold with the expression of a man who has been lost in the desert and has stumbled across an oasis, then he sealed the opening. 'Yep, I guess we'd better go.'

They walked up towards the weir over which the river had swept their companion just the day before. Now the river had turned into a mere stream and they were able to see there was a narrow pass that would take them to the upper reaches of the canyon, and back towards where their horses were tethered.

Due to the fact that three of them – Wattie, Buzz and Ony – were carrying the bags containing their precious cargo, up what was becoming a steep slope, with Davey having to shepherd the two prisoners, one of whom was physically ill, progress was far from quick.

The stony pass beside the weir was the worst spot, because it narrowed to a point where only one person could go through at a time.

'You go first, Wattie,' said Davey, taking over as leader despite the trials he had gone through, or possibly because of them.

'Why me?' asked the sheriff, with a scowl that indicated he was not too happy about being the one to lead the way. Ambush was the unspoken word on all of their minds.

'Well, you're the biggest,' said Davey, 'even though this trip's knocked a bit off that belly, and the second is, I want you to cover me while I get these galoots through.'

Wattie went forward and found that he was in a narrow passage where his body actually touched the sides so that he had to be careful not to rip his clothes on the stony protuberances that plucked at him as he went along. He had to duck his head at one point to avoid hitting the crown on a stone that arched across the way. He was through within a minute or so – it seemed much longer – then moved back and took out his weapon, laying down his burden as he did so. The gold was heavy, even in his dreams he had not thought it would weigh so much, even divided between the three of them.

'All right,' he said loudly, and within another couple of minutes – which seemed forever while he was waiting – out came Hardin, and then Kurzwell, followed closely by Davey, who, being shorter, and a lot more spry than his companions, was close on the heels of his captives, both of whom remained as surly as ever, although Hardin seemed a little brighter and glared at Wattie with baleful eyes that promised a quick revenge if he ever managed to get free of his bonds. Ony came last.

The way before them was grassy, and had been under the river just the day before. This meant that they were constantly sinking into the soggy ground. There was a steep rise too, so Davey had everyone walk inwards against the side of the mountainous hill over which the original settlers had built the rope bridge. Although this way was strewn with pebbles and boulders, it was easier to traverse than the grassland where they felt as if they were walking through molasses.

Wattie, still up front, was the first to top the rise and arrive at the grassy area at the foot of the hills that they had left just the day before. He could see the mesquite and pine trees in front of him where the horses were still tethered from the day before. The animals were a little damp, but they had been sheltered by the trees and the weather had improved considerably in the last day or so.

Now that they had horses to help bear their burden, the party quickened their pace and advanced forward. What a difference a day had made, those twenty-four hours had transformed the river from a roaring torrent to a reasonable body of water. The river still streamed along at a fast pace, but was no longer a major threat now that the waters that had been feeding it had been cut off by the better weather.

Davey and his companions made sure that the horses got some oats to fortify them for the trip, and while they were eating from their nose-bags, Wattie and Ony packed the gold carefully into three different saddle bags. Only Davey's horse was left free from the burden on account of her size.

'Say, this doesn't seem fair,' said Kurzwell as he was being urged up to his own mount. 'You're going to profit from a robbery I didn't take part in. I only helped to take the goods away. I was just a middleman.' Kurzwell looked steadily at Wattie.

'We'll discuss this when we get you back to Benson,' said Wattie.

'Know what?' said Kurzwell rhetorically. 'I think you're planning to do the dirty on them, and that's why you don't want to talk about it. You listening, boys? I think your little sheriff will get in touch with the authorities and you won't see a penny. All this labour for nothing.'

'If you don't shut your mouth I'll shut it for you,' said Wattie mildly. 'Do you want to be gagged for the rest of the trip?'

Kurzwell fell silent, knowing that the sheriff meant exactly what he was saying.

'What's he talking about?' asked Davey, suddenly alert, his head going up as he sniffed the air like a terrier on the scent of a rat.

'Davey, Ony, Buzz, calm it,' said Wattie, 'let's concentrate on getting out of here.'

They at least saw the sense in this. They started crossing the river to get to the bluff beyond which was the passage that led out of the box canyon, within which they were now enclosed. Wattie went first, and now that the swirling tide was down to manageable proportions, he made his way easily despite the extra weight in his saddle bags. Davey took a deep breath, got on his spotted mare and rode over, looking surprised when he was at the other side and still intact. Kurzwell and Hardin rode over in silence while Wattie kept his gun trained on them. They did what was asked of them because neither felt like going for a dip in the still fast-flowing waters.

The group rode around the bluff, but this time with Buzz leading the way as befitted the fact that he was their guide, taking them through the rough ground to the passage which had led them to their ultimate find. They were soon in the area beyond before the river vanished into the bore in the ground. The going was still not easy.

Behind Buzz rode Ony, who had a weapon at his side as he went, while behind him were Kurzwell and Hardin, both of whom exchanged glances as they arrived at the place where the avalanche had occurred. As they passed the area, Buzz and Wattie looked around warily. It was obvious that the thought had occurred to them both that their captives might not have been on their own.

'I see some kind of shelter,' said Buzz, going a little closer, 'but it's wrecked. Hard to tell if there's been anyone there for a while.'

'Well, seeing as there are the remains also of an

avalanche, I guess it's time to keep going,' said Wattie.

By this time the day was wearing on and it was getting towards the early afternoon. The route they had taken was on a steady climb and it was no longer than another hour before they were away from the dangerous place and at the narrow trail that led to Oak Leaf Canyon.

'We'll take it easy here,' said Davey. 'Once we get through we'll kill a few rabbits, fill the water bottles, and set off first thing in the morning. Remember we've got a desert to cross with these two.' He glared at the prisoners as if it was their fault.

'No killings,' said Wattie firmly.

'You'll regret it,' said Davey. 'Anyways, I'm fed up being the last in the string; I'm going first and shooting us some dinner.' With this he took up the head of the train and spurred his horse forward. She obeyed with an indignant snort or two. He was well ahead of the rest and gave a joyful whoop when they emerged at the rocky end and the wide space of Oak Leaf Canyon.

There was crack of a rifle and his wild cry of joy was cut off as Davey fell off his horse and disappeared from sight in the high grass.

CHAPTER SIXTEEN

The three riders from Wattie's group who remained were
laden with the gold, so it was hardly surprising under the
conditions they were in, with the ground still soft in
between the grass, that Kurzwell and his companion were
able to kick the sides of their horses and make off across
the meadow. Ony turned to shoot at them and a bullet
went past his head so closely that it would have taken the
top off if it had been just an inch or two closer. With a
sense of self-preservation that did him justice, that young
man spurred his horse forward, moving faster so he was
much less likely to be hit.

Wattie was not a coward, but he retreated to the rocky
pass out of which they had just emerged for a sound
reason. The lone rifleman had a vantage point within a
series of stony outcrops at the side of the valley. He was
far enough from where the intruders were to shoot at
them, but not close enough to see, concealed as he was
by an upswept ledge. Wattie got off his horse, then,
armed with his gun, came cautiously around the bend.
On foot, in his dark clothing, he was a lesser target for

the gunman.

Wattie's problem was the least of the troubles facing the party. Ony had started his blue forward when the shooting had started and Davey had vanished into the grass. Hardin, who had time to convalesce in his big Western saddle, kicked hard at the flanks of his mount. His horse gave a snort and shot forward, much lighter on its feet than Ony's which was laden down with gold. Letting go of the reins, which he was holding with his good left hand, Hardin struck a paralyzing blow to his enemy's shoulder. Ony gave a gasp of pain and dropped his gun. Hardin managed to get it before it fell to the ground. Another bullet from the rifle just missed Ony's head and he slid from his horse into the long grasses.

'Giddy up!' shouted Hardin and his horse leapt towards the spot from which the shots had come.

In the meantime, Kurzwell took the chance and he too followed in the wake of his employee. Unfortunately for him, he happened to be passing Buzz who flung his body to one side so hard that he unseated both Kurzwell and himself. Buzz was tall and bony while Kurzwell was smaller and more compact. Because they had landed closer to where the gunman was shooting from, the ground was firmer and able to hold their weight. It was at this point that the two men began to engage in a battle royal.

Most probably the instinct for battle is something that is inbred, and cannot be cultivated. Buzz had been brought up in a tough world, but his opponent had learned early on that a man should fight and give no quarter. They began punching each other and Buzz quickly found that the smaller man was light on his feet and able to dodge away from the somewhat heavy-handed attempts of his rival to punch him on the head or jaw. Kurzwell dodged Buzz, and managed to get in three or four punches to the ribs that made the other man gasp in pain.

Buzz made his biggest mistake when he became angry and flustered. He was so annoyed that he tried to punch forward with hammer blows in quick succession, and did not see the thin smile that crossed Kurwell's long face. The criminal knew that when an opponent was rattled this made him even easier to defeat. And so it was with Buzz, because as the smaller man came forward, he kicked Buzz on his knee, a move which knocked the man to the ground. Without a moment's hesitation, he dived forward, grabbed Buzz by his ears, of all things and began to thump his head off the ground. Buzz was soon uncon-scious and bleeding.

Kurzwell let go of the limp body. He was not so blinded by fury that he would not consider his own safety. He ran toward the rocks, carrying the gun he had wrenched from his enemy. As he did so, there was a boom as a Colt .45 was discharged and hit the stony walls in front of him. The bullet bounced back and nearly blew his head off. He turned and Wattie was standing just a few yards away.

'Shoot him, boys,' called out Kurzwell to his compan-ions hidden safely on a ledge.

'Can't,' shouted back Dobbins, speaking for the first time. 'Boss, I've run out of bullets.'

'You idiot, you don't tell them.' Now that particular cat

had leapt out of the bag, Kurzwell had no choice; he took steady aim at Wattie. 'This ain't personal but your buddies are gone and that gold's mine.'

Wattie narrowed his eyes. The trouble was, Kurzwell was still quite distant and he had a smaller, more accurate gun in his hand. Wattie grasped the butt of his weapon with both hands and trusted to pot luck. There was a roar and the Colt jumped in his hands. It was as if the world had slowed down because now he saw that the bullet had missed his enemy completely and ploughed into the plant-life behind him, just missing the bloody body of Buzz. Kurzwell was smiling, if you could call that twisted, evil grimace a smile and Wattie knew beyond certainty that he was a dead man.

'Hey, bastard, you forgot something,' said a grating voice from behind and Kurwell was startled enough to turn his head.

Davey had reared out of the long meadow-grass into which he had fallen. His face was as white as a newly starched collar and his body was hunched forward a little because of an injured shoulder. Wincing with pain, he held up his gun and shot Kurzwell just as the latter was turning to draw on him, but not before Kurzwell had shot at him first.

In his haste the would-be killer missed, but Davey's bullet hit the ex-con square in the chest, where blood blossomed like a red flower. The gunman looked down in some surprise, the expression on his face puzzled as if he had been reminded that he too was mortal. Without another sound, he pitched forward to his face, his limbs quivered and he was still.

154

Davey, job done, his wound too much for his frail body, dropped out of sight again in the long grass.

Wattie ran forward to the escarpment where the other two were hidden. It was a curved ledge that swept up like the brim of sombrero.

As he jumped up, ready to fire at close range, he was met by the unyielding wooden end of a rifle. In his desperation at running out of bullets, Mule was using his Winchester '73 as a club. Luckily it missed Wattie's head, glancing off his shoulder, and the blow was so sweeping that Mule, who had stood up to do so, staggered and fell off the ledge to the ground about six feet below where he lay clutching at his leg and groaning.

Wattie had no time to look at this new enemy. Instead he found Hardin there. But there was something wrong. The big man was on his knees, his wounded arm held in front of him. With a supreme effort he lifted the gun he had taken off Ony and pointed it straight at Wattie. He fired, but the sheriff had seen the move coming because Hardin was so slow. The bullet whistled harmlessly past the standing man, and Wattie ran forward and kicked the gun out of the hand of his enemy. It spun off the ledge to the ground below. Hardin, however, was not finished. Some lumps of basalt had fallen off the rocky walls when the shooting was going on. Hardin grabbed one of these with his good hand and smacked Wattie on the side of the head.

Wattie felt as if he had been hit with a giant hammer. He saw an explosion of white light go off inside his head. He reeled around like a drunk man, knowing inside his head that he had to get away or his skull would be caved in. Hardin struggled to his feet and hit Wattie again. Wattie fell to the ground, blood pouring from a wound on his forehead, and Hardin stood over him, ready to crush Wattie's head in.

'Hated your smug face from the minute we met,' he said.

The sheriff still had the use of his legs. With a desperate strength born of fury, he lifted his not inconsiderable feet and positioned them forward, catching Hardin on his shins. Hardin gave a shout of pain and staggered back, forgetting that behind him there was only open space. Because the ledge curved upwards, he was much higher here than where Mule had fallen off. If he had fallen on the grass that grew right up to the side of the valley, he might only have been winded, but he had only one arm and could not keep his balance. He dropped the rock for a moment; he flailed on the edge, and then fell to the rocks below. He gave a shout of pain, and then there was silence.

Wattie lay there for what seemed like an age, finally getting enough strength to stagger to his feet and look over. Hardin, who had threatened to kill the sheriff, had broken his own skull on the boulders below and was no longer a threat to anyone.

Wattie looked around for his companions.

CHAPTER SEVENTEEN

It was a time to look after your own. Once he had checked that Mule was not a danger to them, Wattie went to help out his friends. He found Davey in the long grass. Davey had suffered a shoulder wound, but luckily the bullet had just grazed him because the undersized cowboy had twisted in the saddle, going with the impact of the bullet as he fell, making the damage much less serious than it might have been. Wattie revived him with some water from the river and led him over to a place where he could sit, a large red stone that stuck out into the grass.

Wattie dressed Davey's wound with some spare cloth from his pack, while Davey swore and cursed under his breath. Wattie made sure the wound was clean.

'By the way, if you try anything,' he told Mule, who lay groaning nearby, 'you'll join your friends.'

He armed Davey with the remaining pistol, and if he had seemed unfriendly before, the black-browed glowering aspect Davey took on now gave him a goblin-like appearance as he guarded their one remaining prisoner.

Wattie searched for, and found Ony, who had been clubbed unconscious by Hardin. Wattie half-carried and half-dragged him to the spot where Davey sat. Ony finally gave a groan and managed to sit up. He took several long draughts of Adam's ale, but Wattie had already gone.

Wattie stood over the body of their guide. He turned as he felt someone standing behind him. It was Ony, who was still swaying slightly.

'The hell with it, just when I was getting to like the old bastard.' He came forward, 'Let's get him cleaned up and give him a decent burial.'

'Him and the other two.'

'I don't give a shit about them.'

'Yes, but the wild animals around here will,' said Wattie. 'Which is why I'm going to get started right now.' He bent over the bloody body, and then stood up. 'Ony, give me a hand.'

'I'll do my best.'

'Let's get him cleaned up, and nursed.'

'What in the name of Jehoshaphat d'you mean?'

'He's still breathing, Ony.'

Three days later, five men got ready for the long journey across the desert. They had filled plenty of skins with water, and had bags stuffed full of meadow grass for their horses. Mule, not having a lying bone in his body, told them the truth about Kurzwell and Hardin, and agreed to help them. In exchange, they would look after him even though he had caused them so much trouble.

Ony had been a remarkable help concerning the care

given to his brother. He had helped to dress the wounds caused by Kurzwell, cursing Buzz all the time for the risks he had taken.

'You better not die on me, you old bastard, after taking all this trouble,' he said.

Wattie had dug the graves for the two dead men almost single-handed since he was the fittest of the four, with Ony lending a helping hand as he recovered from the blow that had knocked him out, and on a break from tending his brother. Wattie had even made a kind of cairn for the buried men, covering them in rocks, of which there were plenty.

Ony had questioned the reason for this because they were both exhausted by the time they came to end of their task, but Wattie had pointed out to him that the cougars, the bears and the coyotes who lived in the valley were not averse to some fresh meat and the party didn't want to attract any more predators, since the human ones had been bad enough.

That night, in a different cave from the one that had sheltered them from the rains, while the animals remained tethered to the trees, the men all sat around a campfire.

'When we get back I'm going to see Dolores,' said Ony. 'She's a good kid, I'm sorry for what I did to her. She might have me back.'

Wattie produced the bottle of whiskey, which had somehow survived the trauma of the last few days hidden in his effects.

'At least we got something out of this.' The party shared out the drink, except strangely, for Buzz. As the bottle was passed to him he shook his head.

'No,' he said, 'I'm done for with that stuff, you guys. Its coffee and sarsaparilla for me from now on. I'll have a business to run.' And he meant it.

Now it was time for them to go. Davey faced the sheriff with a glittering eye as they made their way towards the head of Oak Leaf Canyon.

'Well, Sheriff, are you going to play the dirty on us? Or are we going to stay friends?'

Wattie looked at him and thought of all that gold that would lie useless in government vaults if it was declared on their arrival. Then he thought of his beautiful wife and the things he could give her.

'We'll see,' he said.

They rode out under azure blue skies to a desert that would take them days to cross. They were no longer riders in the storm.

The storms had passed away.

For the moment.

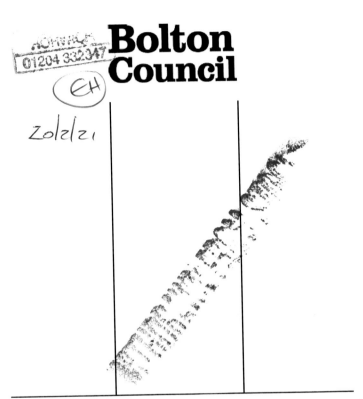

Bolton Council

Please return / renew this item
by the last date shown.
Books may also be renewed by
phone or the Internet.

Tel: 01204 332384

www.bolton.gov.uk/libraries